SEPTEMBER ISLAND

By Rosalie Fry

SEPTEMBER
ISLAND

by
Rosalie Fry

Illustrated by
Margery Gill

NEW YORK: E. P. Dutton & Co., Inc.

3361

SEPTEMBER ISLAND

CHAPTER 1

'MARTIN?'

'Mmmm.'

'Oh, Martin, I do wish you wouldn't always say "Mmmm" when I want to talk to you!' The small girl rolled over as she spoke and raised a reproachful face over the edge of the bunk in which she was already settled for the night. Her brother looked up from his book and said severely:

'Now look here, Linda, you aren't supposed to be talking at all. You know perfectly well that Mummy said she'd only go across to the Palmers' this evening if you were good and went to sleep properly.'

'Don't want her to go to the Palmers',' mumbled Linda.

'How dare you say such a thing!' cried Martin fiercely. 'Poor Mum's done nothing but cook and see to things here in

7

the trailer all day; you ought to be glad for her to have some fun.'

'But she *did* have some fun,' said Linda in an aggrieved tone. 'We played games all the time it rained. And she won three times,' she added thoughtfully.

Martin sighed, reminding himself that Linda was only six, and couldn't be expected to understand that grown-up people sometimes found such games as ludo rather boring, even if they did win.

He himself was eleven, and in many ways seemed older. His father, an army officer, had lately been posted to Singapore, and before leaving had remarked:

'Well, Martin, you'll be the man of the family now, so it will be up to you to take good care of that little mother of yours, and see that your lively young sister doesn't get out of hand while I'm away.'

Martin took this trust very seriously, and was so anxious to look after his mother properly that he soon learned to shoulder responsibilities far beyond his years.

After watching him through her lashes Linda tried a new approach.

'Ben's got up on your bunk,' she warned. 'And we forgot to take his coat off.'

Hearing his name the little black dachshund rolled a watchful eye in their direction. He was not an active dog, preferring beds to walks any day of the week. He was only waiting now to slither under the bedclothes when nobody was looking! He considered this holiday trailer a poor substitute for home, and hated the long wet grass that took the place of the town pavements to which he was accustomed.

Linda sighed and tried again.

'I'm awfully hungry,' she announced, sitting up in her bunk. Martin took no notice.

Ben seized his opportunity and slid noiselessly under the blankets until only the tip of his black tail could be seen on the pillow.

'I'm hungry,' repeated Linda a little more clearly.

'Oh no, you're not; you go to sleep,' said Martin firmly. 'Anyway, you've cleaned your teeth.'

'I could clean them again,' she pointed out.

'You know very well we're short of water,' he retorted. 'Besides, it's only an excuse to put off going to sleep, *I* know!'

'It isn't,' insisted Linda. 'I'm so hungry that I feel sort of sick when I lie down.'

Martin became exasperated.

'Now look here, Lin, are you going to sleep, or do I have to call across to Mummy like she said?'

Linda subsided without another word. With a sigh of relief Martin reached out for a tattered army haversack hanging above his bunk.

This haversack was his most treasured possession, since it held the equipment for the adventurous expeditions for which he was always preparing. He now undid the buckles and, opening the haversack, emptied the contents on to the table under the window. There were maps and lists and a notebook, and an old hip-flask of his father's, also string and wire and pliers, and best of all a compass—the mere sight of its tremulous needle was enough to set him dreaming of adventure in far places.

For a while Linda lay listening to the familiar sounds as

9

Martin got out his equipment. When she was absolutely certain that there was no hope of having any fun with her brother she rolled over to face the wall. Then, dragging a limp and almost hairless teddy bear from the depths of the blankets, she launched into a long whispered conversation, a sure sign that she and Brown Teddy were off on one of the never-ending imaginary adventures that kept her happy for hours on end.

In the bunk beyond, deep under the stifling bedclothes, another dream-adventure was beginning, for Ben was having a nightmare! It was clear from his strangled yelps that this was no dream of cushioned beds and city streets, but something so exciting that the mounded bedclothes heaved as his short legs twitched in a frantic attempt to run.

Meanwhile, at the table under the window, plans for the biggest adventure of all were steadily taking shape. For although this was, as yet, as much of a dream-adventure as those of Ben and Linda, Martin was perfectly certain that some day, some-how, all his preparations would lead him into a truly wonderful and entirely real adventure.

For as long as he could remember he had planned to be an explorer, and whenever Major Roberts was home on leave he helped Martin with his equipment, and taught him the sort of things that explorers need to know. Although not an explorer himself, he knew enough about travelling to give his son some useful tips. He was a wise man too, and, while encouraging the boy's interest, he did not allow him to get the idea that ex-ploring was all adventure and excitement.

'There's any amount of real hard work, much of it extremely dull,' he had warned. 'And often hardship and danger into the bargain. But in the best exploring there's something else as well. For when you win through to your objective, whether it be the source of a river or a mountain top or a small uncharted island, your discovery sometimes turns out to be even better than you expected. And when that happens you'll have a moment of delight to treasure all your life.'

After this conversation Martin worked harder than ever over his preparations, determined that his own expeditions should lead to that moment of delight.

But so far he had not had much opportunity for adventure of any kind. To begin with it would be hard to imagine a less exciting place than the town in which he lived. If only it had been a riverside town, with wharves and warehouses and shipping, or a town of alley-ways and ruins where anything might happen! But it wasn't that kind of place at all; it was simply a pretty suburban town of trim crescents and new housing developments, where every tree was grown for decoration, not for climbing. It was impossible to imagine anyone having a real adventure in such a district.

Small wonder, then, that the trailer holiday promised to be the most exciting event of Martin's life, especially as the surrounding countryside included everything that an explorer's heart could wish for—sea, rivers, woods and sandhills—all within walking distance of their base camp.

It's true the trailer itself was in a field with seven others, but the field was situated on the crown of a low headland, and one had only to walk out to the end of this head to command the whole sweep of a sandy estuary through which a river wound its way to the sea. A smaller tributary flowed into the estuary from a wooded valley just below the headland, and, although this creek could not be seen from the hilltop, Martin knew he had only to run down through the woods to find himself on its banks. Just to think of it filled his head with visions.

/ But these dreams were not to be realized straight away. To begin with, they had a good deal of rain, and since there was nowhere to dry their clothes they simply had to stay indoors to avoid getting everything wet.

They also discovered that every job took longer to do in a trailer than in the house at home; bunks proved harder to make than beds, cooking was awkward in the confined space and every drop of water had to be fetched in cans. Shopping was difficult too, especially for anyone accustomed to the chain stores in town which delivered everything, and Martin found himself making countless trips to the one small shop for things that had been forgotten.

So here they were, at the end of the third day already, and still Martin had not explored the creek, although he had worked out the main direction of its course with map and compass. He spread this map on the table now, and was tracing the river back to its source in the hills, when the trailer gave an unexpected lurch. This was followed by a sound of scrabbling as someone climbed on to the tow bar outside. He looked up just as a face was pressed against the window. It was a freckled face, with a faint pink moustache suggesting a recent drink of raspberryade. Martin recognized the boy known to his friends as Rocky. He had often noticed the group about the camp.

Now, from various bumps and scuffles, he guessed that several other members of the gang were collected under the window, although he could not see them from where he sat.

After a hasty glance at the equipment on the table, Rocky jumped down from the bar and made his way round to the

open door of the trailer. Martin got up and went out to meet
his visitors. He now saw that the whole gang was there, seven
of them, all boys round about his own age. Rocky was evidently
the leader, and he now acted as spokesman for the group.

'Hi-yer!' he remarked cheerfully. 'We saw your old woman going out, so it seemed a good time to come over.'

Martin stiffened. He had never before heard his mother referred to as his 'old woman' and he didn't like it. He didn't like it at all. However he said nothing, since it was evident that Rocky intended to be friendly, as was proved by his next remark.

'This is the Adventure Club,' he announced, introducing his companions with a wave of the hand. 'We've been watching you, and we've decided you can join our club if you like.'

Martin flushed with pleasure at this exciting invitation, but Rocky's next words dashed his hopes.

'We're going to have a meeting in our hide-out now—like to come along and be enrolled?'

Martin swallowed uncomfortably.

'I'm afraid I can't come just now,' he confessed in a low voice. 'I've got to look after my kid sister.'

'Oh, I see, a baby-sitter, tough luck!' said Rocky. 'Oh, well, so long then! Maybe we might enrol you another day—not tomorrow though, because we've got a special expedition fixed for tomorrow.' And with a shrill whistle to his followers he was gone.

Martin watched them disappear into the woods where they held their meetings, wondering whether he might have gone on tomorrow's expedition if only he had been free to join them now. He climbed back into the trailer and slumped down at the table, where even the sight of his precious compass failed to raise his spirits. His preparations seemed to be leading nowhere and the 'moment of delight' seemed far away indeed. Never in all his life had he longed for a real adventure so

14

desperately badly. And never had adventure seemed quite so far away.

'Martin!' Linda's voice startled him in the quietness of the trailer. 'Martin, let's have an adventure of our own; we could have a much better one than those boys, I know we could, you and me and Brown Teddy and Ben.'

'You'd better get to sleep before Mum comes back,' advised Martin, speaking a good deal more severely than he intended. He hadn't the heart to explain that nobody could have a real adventure with a spoilt little girl of six, a teddy bear and a fat town dog in a coat!

CHAPTER 2

NEXT day was warm and sunny. As soon as the morning jobs were done and the water fetched, Mrs Roberts turned to Martin.

'Well now, I expect you'd like to be off to explore that creek of yours while I get lunch,' she suggested. 'Those two little girls from the Dormobile have taken Linda off to play, so there's only Ben. He might like to go with you perhaps.'

'Honestly, Mum, can you imagine poor old Benbow exploring anything!' laughed Martin. 'He'd probably expect to be carried! I'll put his cushion out here on the grass where he can lie in the sun.'

He made the little dog comfortable and then set off, unaware that two brown eyes were following him as he made for the gap through which he had seen the Adventurers enter the wood the previous evening.

16

He was soon following a narrow track down through the tangled undergrowth, which grew shoulder-high in places. At the start this track ran steeply down the densely wooded hill-side. Then, with an unexpected twist, it swung sharply away to the right, where it disappeared under a tree so overgrown with clustering ivy that its weighted branches dipped to the ground. Lifting aside this curtain of greenery, Martin crept underneath.

He found himself in a cavern so dark that at first he couldn't see a thing. He stumbled against the roots of the tree, and, feeling these with his hands, found one that formed a convenient seat. He sat on this, and as his eyes became accustomed to the dim light he saw that he was in a leafy cave. The earth floor was trampled flat and swept clear of leaves, whilst the tree-roots were smooth as though polished by constant use. There was a strange air of occupation about the place, and suddenly he wondered if this was the hide-out that Rocky had mentioned. The discovery of a spearmint chewing-gum wrapper confirmed this guess, and he sighed with longing to be a member of such a clubroom.

His sigh was echoed by a snuffle, and he became aware of the sound of a heavy body blundering down through the under-growth outside. There was another snuffle, followed by a satisfied snort as Ben edged in under the curtain of ivy.

'Oh, Ben, why ever did you have to follow me?' he exclaimed in annoyance.

Ben wagged a jaunty tail, looking quite delighted with himself.

'Go home, Ben, *home*!' ordered Martin, pointing up through the trees.

Ben wagged his tail again. It was obvious that he had no intention of obeying. There was worse to follow.

'Mar—tin!' Linda's voice rang out plaintively from somewhere higher up the wood. Ben barked sharply, then stood with his head cocked expectantly.

'Sh! Ben, shut up, for goodness' sake,' hissed Martin. 'We don't want her tagging after us, she'll ruin everything. She's much better up there with the Dormobile kids.'

'Martin, where are you?' There was an ominous hint of tears in the voice this time. Martin pushed out into the sunlight with a scowl.

Linda was trailing down through the wood dragging Brown Teddy by the arm. Her face was streaked with tears and she had hiccups.

'Now what's wrong?' he demanded impatiently. 'I thought you were supposed to be playing with the Dormobile kids.'

'I hate them,' said Linda with a sob.

'You're thoroughly spoilt, that's what's the matter with you,' said Martin sternly. 'Why must you always quarrel with everyone?'

'They wouldn't let me have a turn with the truck and it wasn't fair,' she quavered. 'So then I wanted to come with you and now you're horrid too.'

'Well if I'm so horrid why don't you stay with Mummy?' he demanded.

'Mummy doesn't w-w-want me either, she's busy cooking the dinner and she wants me out in the sun.' The tears began to flow again.

'Nobody's going to want you if you snivel like that,' he retorted. 'Oh, well, as you're here I suppose I'll have to take you along. But you're not to be a nuisance. Understand?'

'Mmmm.'

18

'And you'll have to look after yourself. I'm exploring, so I can't hold every bramble out of your way or lift you over things, is that clear?'

'Yes,' nodded Linda. She was cheering up already.

Martin turned and plunged off down the hillside, going a good deal faster than he need have done in his determination not to be held back. He could hear Linda stumbling after him, keeping up as well as her short legs would allow. The one who did not keep up was Ben. He sat down and whimpered miserably the moment he found himself faced by a thicket of tangled bracken.

'Now don't you start!' warned Martin. 'I never asked you to come, remember.'

He was secretly amused to hear his warning echoed in an undertone by Linda.

'Shush, Ben!' she hissed. 'Be quiet or he'll make us go back.'

To Martin's surprise the whimpering stopped immediately, and out of the side of his eye he saw Linda come struggling down through the trees with Ben clasped in her arms, his long body dangling to within an inch or two of the ground. Brown Teddy was held between her teeth by a tattered ear.

Martin's heart relented. Poor Lindy, she could be quite a game little kid at times, and, after all, he supposed it really wasn't her fault if she was spoilt. He waited for her to catch up.

'I should put him down now,' he suggested kindly. 'He can easily manage this bit. Come along, Benbow, there's a good dog.'

'It's only because he doesn't understand about the country, you know; he isn't a sissy really,' said Linda loyally, allowing the heavy dog to slither awkwardly out of her arms. He picked himself up with a business-like shake and set off down the hill with no more fuss, his tail waving cheerfully as though he had suddenly decided it was going to be rather fun being a tough country dog for a change.

'Don't his paws sound different here in the woods?' said Linda. 'At home they go scritch-scritch-scritch on the pavements, but here it's only pad-pad-pad. I like it.'

'Listen!' cried Martin, raising his head suddenly. 'That must be the river. Come on!'

Linda took his outstretched hand with a radiant smile.

'Is this going to be an adventure?' she inquired.

Although Martin had been dreaming about the creek for days he had not expected to find it such an enchanting place. The little river ran through a deeply wooded gorge which widened as it neared the estuary. At the point where he and Linda ran out of the woods the bank sloped to a shelving beach where seaweed draped the rocks, proof of the salt sea tides that swept up and down the river twice a day.

On the opposite bank was a similar beach. Behind it the woods had been cut back just enough to make room for a solitary house. It was an old, haphazard building, and some of its walls were washed with pink, whilst others showed the original stone of which the place was built. One such wall rose directly from the beach, its lower portion buttressed to withstand the force of the tides. This wall was stained with green slime to within a few feet of the lower windows.

'What a wonderful house to live in,' said Martin. 'You could lean out when the tide was high and touch a boat sailing past your window.'

At the moment there was no sign of life, either in the house itself or in the narrow garden that stretched between the beach and the encroaching woods. However, there were curtains at the windows and some washing flapped on a line at the back, showing that the place was at least inhabited.

On their own side of the river they could see two other buildings, a red-roofed cottage upstream to their right and the chimneys of another amongst the trees to their left. This second cottage stood directly above the point where the small river joined the estuary.

'Let's go there first,' suggested Martin. 'I want to see where this creek runs into the main river.'

He turned and led the way along the tree-bordered river bank. In many places the high tides had washed away large lumps of earth, exposing the trees' great roots until they twisted above the rocks like tangled snakes. One such tree stood like a sentinel on the extreme end of a little promontory that ran out into the river at the point where the creek joined the estuary. Around this promontory the force of the water had swept away so much of the bank that it had scooped out a considerable cave right under the tree itself.

'It's just like a darling little house in here, with the walls all made of tree roots,' called Linda, crawling inside with Brown Teddy tucked under one arm. Ben snuffled at her heels, determined not to miss anything.

But Martin had discovered something else. The far side of the promontory curved to form a rocky cove facing the wide sweep of the estuary itself, and at the top of this cove, close under the bank, stood a simple boat-house falling into ruin. He went round to the front and pulled open the rickety door. To

his astonishment he saw that the shed still housed a dilapidated boat.

To the town-bred boy it was unbelievable that anyone should have abandoned such a treasure. But the reason was not far to seek. Climbing up the bank above the cove he came upon the cottage whose chimneys he had noticed among the trees. He now saw that it was empty, and indeed little more than a hollow shell, the wilderness of its neglected garden all but obliterating the broken windows and swinging door.

'Yet it must have been a grand home once,' he mused, turning to look back on the wide view over the estuary. It was strange to realize that people had lived and worked here not so long ago. Perhaps a boy like himself used to run down the slope to launch the old boat from its shed on the shore, just as he himself would dearly love to do.

He wandered down to look at it again. The sagging roof of the shed had let in enough rain to collect in a pool in the bottom of the boat, and this had prevented the warped timbers from drying out entirely. He climbed into the boat and sat on the forward thwart, gazing through the open door to the wide curve of the river, trying to imagine how it would feel to set off on a voyage of discovery in such a boat as this.

After studying the far bank of the river his gaze returned to the near shore and the sentinel pine on the promontory. Remembering Linda he looked amongst its roots, and was surprised to see her still crouching in the cave where he had left her. Her face was pressed to a gap between the roots, for all the world as though she were looking out of a window, and from the tenseness of her attitude it was clear that something was holding all her attention. Sliding over the edge of the boat he walked across the cove to join her.

'What's up, Lin?' he questioned, stooping down in the entrance to her cave.

Without removing her eye from the opening Linda groped behind her with a hand, and pulled him down beside her.

'There's a witch over there in the garden,' she informed him hoarsely, still keeping her eyes on the old house on the far side of the creek.

'Don't be silly, witches are only in fairy tales,' he laughed.

'This one isn't,' insisted Linda. 'And there's a girl too. I think she must be a young witch, because she's got black hair all pouring down her back. And they've got a cat each, like witches always have—the old witch has a black one and the young witch has a ginger one. I expect the old witch is cruel to her and that's why she's hiding.'

Martin was about to make a teasing reply when a figure moved across the garden and startled him into silence. She was old and bent and dressed in black, except for a wide-brimmed garden hat which perched incongruously on her snow-white hair. There was no doubt about it, she did look like a witch, and to add to the impression a black cat stalked beside her with his tail straight up in the air. But he was clearly no ordinary cat; he was almost as large as Ben, and like Ben he wore a collar round his neck, allowing the old lady to lead him around the garden like a dog on the end of a leash. The strange pair circled the lawn slowly before returning to the house. Only then did Martin find his voice.

'I don't see any girl,' he said.

'She's up in the tree,' said Linda.

Martin turned his attention to a tree that stood on the extreme edge of the garden bank, its branches overhanging the water. Despite the width of the river he could see that it was laden with yellow pears.

Suddenly two long legs in blue jeans dangled down through the leaves, and a moment later a girl dropped from the lower branches and turned towards the house. She had, as Linda had said, a cloud of long dark hair. Under one arm she carried a yellow cat. Martin judged her to be about his own age. He was intrigued to see that she carried a haversack like his own,

24

swinging it by the long strap as she strolled across the narrow lawn.

With a sudden twist the cat sprang out of her arms and streaked towards the house. As the girl clutched her haversack and darted after it Martin turned to Linda with a smile.

'Not much wrong with her, witch or no witch,' he remarked.

But he had no sooner spoken than the girl's voice, sharp with fear, rang out across the water:

'Oh no—no—NO!' she screamed. With a wild leap she shot into the house, a door slammed and there was silence.

CHAPTER 3

MARTIN was every bit as interested as Linda now, and he crouched beside her in the tree-root cave, waiting for a further sign of life from the mysterious house across the water. But when nothing further happened he began to be aware of his cramped position, and backed out on to the shore, glad to stretch his legs and stand upright again. Ben followed, shaking himself so vigorously that his ears flapped over his head with a loud leathery sound.

'Let's go up the creek a bit,' suggested Martin. 'We can keep an eye on your witch's house as we go along. But I do want to see that other cottage too, the one all covered in creeper. Come, Ben.'

Linda was so absorbed in her witch's house that she might even have forgotten poor Brown Teddy if Martin hadn't picked him up and pushed him into her hands as she crawled out from amongst the roots. She was far too preoccupied to look where she was going, and stumbled so often on the uneven bank that Martin was forced to take her hand to prevent her falling.

'The witch must have locked her in somewhere,' she murmured, her eyes wide and solemn. However, there was nothing further to be seen or heard, and as the cottage came into view it caught her interest in spite of herself.

It was a funny little place, so smothered in flowers and creepers that it appeared to be part of the bank on which it stood. Its steep little garden ran right down to the water's edge, where flowers overflowed the low wall to dip their petals into the river. Deep among the flowers Martin spotted a rounded object that he took at first for an old straw beehive such as he had seen in pictures. A curious humming added to this impression. But as they came nearer the humming stopped and the object moved, and he saw that it was a battered straw hat. Its owner turned in their direction, proving to be a little old man with the bluest eyes the children had ever seen. These eyes crinkled up in welcome now, and he called out:

'You wanting the ferry?'

'Oh no, thank you, we were only looking at your garden,' answered Martin.

'Why, come you in then and welcome,' said the old man, hurrying to the gate to greet them. 'My name's Joseph—Old Joseph, on account of my son's being Young Joseph. I works the ferry here since I retired from the sea.'

As he spoke he nodded to the bottom of the garden, where a stout little boat bobbed at the foot of a steep flight of steps.

'D'you mean you row people backwards and forwards across the river like a—well, like a sort of bus?' questioned Martin, who had never seen a ferry before.

'That's right. Saves folks going all the way up to the bridge, you see, a good mile up the creek that is, and no decent road on this side, neither.'

'How do you know when people want to cross?' asked Martin.

'Well, on this side of the river they looks over the gate, same as you looked over yourself,' the old man explained. 'And on the other side I've hung a ship's bell in the thorn tree—see it there by the path?'

Following the direction of his pointing finger they could just make out the glimmer of polished brass in the shadows under the branches. But now his attention returned to his visitors.

'Tell me now, would you be liking plums I wonder?' he asked.

'Ooh yes!' cried Linda.

'Please,' added Martin automatically.

Even Ben seemed to sense that food had been mentioned and wagged his tail hopefully.

The plums were pink and yellow Victorias, growing on a tree against the cottage wall. The old man selected the ripest, picking two for Martin and two for Linda. Ben whined softly in the back of his throat.

'That dog's never wanting a plum, for goodness' sake?' laughed the old man.

'I'm afraid he likes absolutely everything as long as it's food; he's terribly greedy really,' said Martin apologetically. 'All right, Ben, be quiet, here's a bit of mine, but that's all you're having.'

'Ah, no, let him have one for himself, poor creature, we've plenty as you can see,' insisted their host, reaching up for another plum.

'I'll take out the stone for him, shall I?' suggested Linda.

'He gobbles so fast I'm afraid he might bite on it by mistake and hurt his poor teeth.'

They were still licking the stickiness from their fingers when a sputtering sound attracted their attention, and looking across the river they saw a scarlet motor scooter bounding down the uneven lane that led to the witch's house. Here the rider dismounted and wheeled the machine into an outbuilding, reappearing a moment later without it.

'Somehow I wouldn't have thought they'd have a motor scooter there,' said Martin in surprise.

Old Joseph chuckled.

'Ah, the Challenors like my Janet,' he said proudly. 'They've always allowed her to keep her scooter in their garage.'

'Janet?' repeated Linda. 'But Janet's a girl's name,' and she stared doubtfully at the striding figure in slacks and duffel coat, topped by a white and scarlet crash helmet.

'Ay, that's my Janet. She's a reporter, see, works on the local paper. She's a clever lass, is Janet, and a good lass too, looks after her old dad a treat, she does. But now she'll be ringing the bell for me to fetch her over.'

He hurried down the garden, reaching the steps just as the deep note of the bell clanged out across the water. Martin and Linda followed and stood on the bottom step, watching him untie the painter and reach for his oars. He was about to push off when something in Martin's expression caught his attention.

'Care to come over with me?' he invited. 'There's plenty of room for the pair of you, and the dog as well if you like.'

Before he so much as finished speaking Martin was in the boat, with Linda close on his heels. Even Ben jumped in without waiting to be helped.

29

'I never went in a boat before,' said Linda excitedly.

'I've been once, on the Serpentine, when Daddy took me to London,' said Martin. 'But that was only a pleasure trip. This is a much more real kind of boat because it's a working boat of course.'

'I like working boats,' said Linda.

30

As he pulled out from the bank the old man glanced up-stream.

'The migrants'll soon be off,' he observed, jerking his head towards a great flock of birds picking their way across the wet

mud at the foot of the river bank. 'They always gather here for a last feed in the estuary before they take off at this time of year.'

'Where do they go?' asked Linda, turning to watch a sand-piper skim out over the water in a wide arc, whistling softly as it flew.

'Oh, south,' said the old man vaguely. 'Africa maybe; I'm not sure. But away from these shores anyway, more's the pity. Some stay here all winter, of course, but most of that lot will be gone in a few days now. I always miss them when they go.'

'What kind of birds are they?' Martin asked.

'Well, there's a good few different birds out there just now; dunlin, sandpipers, ringed plovers, curlew. I fancy there's a couple of whimbrel too. I'll be able to see for sure when we get closer.'

Martin, knowing only the still waters of the Serpentine, was surprised to see Old Joseph steer for a point well above the wooden step on which his daughter was waiting. She, however, made no move to go upstream to meet them, and it was soon clear that the course had been set purposely to counteract the force of the strong current. As a result the final pull on the oars brought the nose of the boat right in to the step, where Janet stooped to hold it steady, waiting for the children to get out.

'Oh, these aren't passengers,' her father explained. 'They're staying above in the trailer camp, and have only come over and back for the trip. They don't get much chance of boating where they come from.'

As soon as Janet was settled in the boat she pulled off her crash helmet, and they saw that she was not only a girl, but a young and pretty one.

'How long are you going to be home this time?' asked her father, using one oar to steady the boat, while the current swung it slowly round.

'Oh, not much more than an hour. I've to report on a wedding at twelve, and then go on to Whitchurch to cover the races. And I'd like to look in on a hundredth birthday party as well if I've time.'

'And what about Miss Challenor—any news of her today?' he inquired as he started to row.

'Oh yes, I called at the hospital on my way through this morning. I hadn't time to go in and see her, but they say she had a good night and is getting along very well, thank goodness."

'Is Miss Challenor the old witch we saw in the garden?' asked Linda before Martin could prevent her. But to his relief Janet only laughed.

'Oh no, indeed!' she exclaimed. 'No one could possibly call Miss Challenor a witch! I expect it was her old mother you

32

saw. I suppose you *might* think she looked a bit like a witch, especially if she had that cat at her heels! Poor old lady, though, she'll be quite lost without her daughter to keep things going, I'm afraid. That's really why I've dashed home now; there'll just be time for me to run up some little cakes to help them out. I simply can't imagine what they'll be living on.'

'Good thing it was nothing worse than appendicitis, so Miss Challenor won't be away too long,' observed her father. 'I can't see old Mrs C. able to keep things going over there on her own for long.'

'But she wasn't on her own, we saw a girl there too,' said Linda.

'Ah yes, Alex. She's Miss Challenor's goddaughter; she often spends a week or so here in the holidays. But I doubt she'd be much help in a crisis, always got her head in the clouds or her nose in a book!' laughed Janet. 'She's a nice kid though,' she went on. 'I'm very fond of Alex. She means to be a writer, although she doesn't tell that to everyone, for fear of getting laughed at. Her tiresome brothers will tease her about her writing, insisting she'll never get anything published. However, she tells me she's starting a new book in spite of them. It's to be called *The Ferryman's Daughter* and I am to be the heroine —without my scooter and helmet though. Alex finds those very unromantic, I'm afraid!'

'I don't suppose she gets much chance to write at that boarding-school of hers,' observed Old Joseph.

'She gets precious little chance anywhere, as far as I can see,' said Janet. 'Unfortunately Miss Challenor thinks it's a waste of time; she'd far rather see her playing around with other kids.'

'You'd think she'd enough of kids in term time,' remarked her father thoughtfully.

'I know,' said Janet with a sigh. 'And the pity of it is she really writes quite well, if only they'd give her a chance to get on with it. People are so inclined to be discouraging, and Alex is one who needs to be boosted, not discouraged.'

Linda gave a heartfelt sigh.

'I knew they were cruel to her,' she said solemnly. 'She was chasing after her cat and we heard her give a simply awful screech. And then somebody banged the door like THAT!' She clapped her hands so loudly as she spoke that a small party of dunlin rose from the mudbank in alarm and flickered away out of sight round the bend of the river.

'Poor old Alex!' said Janet with a little laugh. 'I was afraid they'd have trouble with those cats without Miss Challenor there to control them. You see the big black fellow is a newcomer, just strolled in one day from nobody knows where, and settled down like the lord of the manor! No wonder poor old Ginger flies at him whenever he gets the chance! Miss Challenor manages to keep them apart, shutting one up while she feeds the other and so on. But the old lady and Alex aren't up to all their tricks, of course; they've had one frightful fight already, Alex tells me.'

'So she isn't locked up in a dungeon after all!' said Linda in such a disappointed tone that everybody laughed.

The moment the boat touched her home shore Janet jumped out on to the steps, and having hastily secured the painter to its ring, she flew up the steps, two at a time, calling back over her shoulder as she went:

'Sorry to fly like this, but if I'm not quick I'll never get those cakes made before it's time to dash out again.'

34

Martin and Linda followed more slowly with Old Joseph.

'We'll have to be going too, I'm afraid,' said Martin regretfully. 'Else Mum will be getting worried, wondering where we are.'

'Ah, that's right,' said the old man. Then, turning to glance up at the sky he added:

'There'll be a storm afore long, you mark my words. I don't like the feel of the day at all.'

'Yet it looks so calm and peaceful, doesn't it?' murmured Martin, his eyes following a fluffy seed of thistledown as it drifted by on the breeze.

'Can't go by looks, you can't. See them birds up there? They know what's coming right enough,' and the old man nodded towards a twittering group lining the telegraph wires above their heads.

'What are they? Swallows!' asked Martin.

'Oh no, that lot's martins. Sand-martins.'

'Martins?' echoed Linda. 'Are there really birds called martins?'

'Course there are!' smiled Old Joseph. 'And grand little travellers they are too, flying all the way to South Africa for the winter. How's that for adventure, and themselves no longer than your hand?'

Martin stared up at the birds with increased interest.

'Seems as though anyone named after them would simply have to be a traveller too, doesn't it?' he mused.

'Ay, couldn't hardly be a better name for a traveller than Martin, could there?' the old man agreed.

CHAPTER 4

A JAGGED flash of lightning zigzagged across the window, followed by a crash of thunder that shook the trailer. Martin raised his head from the pillow, and in the flash that followed he saw Ben's bright eyes watching him from the corner where he slept. Seeing that somebody was awake the little dog slid off his cushion, and still trailing the small blue blanket in which he had been wrapped he pattered across the floor, to bounce up against the side of Martin's bunk, wagging his tail and whining excitedly in hopes of a little midnight fun and attention.

'Hush, Ben! You'll wake Linda if you make such a noise,' whispered Martin reprovingly.

But Ben had no intention of giving in without another try, so he whined again, more loudly than before.

In desperation Martin reached down, and gripping him firmly by the scruff of the neck hoisted him on to his bunk. This was exactly what Ben had hoped for, and he promptly burrowed down under the blankets, very well pleased with the way things had turned out.

Again the room was flooded with light, and soon the first heavy drops of rain began to spatter on the roof. Martin heard his mother stir, but Linda didn't move.

It was the longest thunderstorm Martin ever remembered; it must have been an hour or more before it finally grumbled into silence among the hills.

And then the rain, which had seemed heavy enough before, began in sober earnest, roaring down with such concentrated force that it seemed as though the thin roof above their heads must be battered in. And instead of the short, sharp shower that usually follows a thunderstorm, this rain went on hour after hour without any sign of a let-up. Even Linda woke for a moment, raising a tousled head to babble something about 'lots of rain' before burrowing down again.

But the noise was so tremendous that Martin found it impossible to sleep, even under the bedclothes, and when he tried to speak he couldn't make his mother hear him above the uproar. He slid out of bed and went across to her.

'Shall I make some tea, Mum?' he shouted. 'It's so dull just lying doing nothing.'

'Good idea,' said his mother. 'Don't wake Linda, though. Here, hang this scarf over the light so that it won't disturb her.'

After draping the light Martin filled the kettle and lit the gas. The ring of flame made a cheerful spot of colour in the darkened room. He could not hear the sound of the kettle singing above the storm, but the spurt of steam showed him when it was ready.

'Oh dear, the milk's gone sour!' he exclaimed.

'Ah, that's the thunder of course,' said his mother; 'Never mind, there's a bottle of lemon juice in the cupboard, let's have a dash of that instead, and plenty of sugar. That should help us to sleep.'

Linda didn't stir again, but the clink of cups, faint though it was, was enough to bring Ben nosing out from the depths of Martin's bunk.

'There you are, old greedy!' laughed Martin, pouring the last dregs into his saucer, and adding an extra sprinkle of sugar before putting it down on the floor.

But poor old Ben discovered that once out of bed he was expected to stay there, and although he rolled his eyes hopefully towards the bunk, Martin took no notice, but settled him

on his cushion in the corner, tucking his own little blanket firmly round him before getting back into the bunk himself.

The rain went on and on without a break until the very steadiness of the sound lulled them to sleep at last.

When next they woke it was morning, and the rain was still drumming on the roof. Martin got up and went to the window. He found himself looking on to an astonishing scene. The field in which the trailers stood was flooded to a depth of several inches, and coloured plastic pails and other movable equipment lay floating amongst the wheels. One or two people were out already, sloshing about in raincoats and boots, retrieving their scattered property and examining the trailers for signs of damage.

Martin flung on his clothes and slipped outside himself. He soon came across Rocky stumping about with a bucket in his hand.

'Hi!' he called on seeing Martin. 'Seen the estuary this morning?'

'No, why?'

'River's changed its course on account of the storm, twice as much water as usual coming down and all sorts of queer things floating in it, farm gates, chicken coops, whole trees, roots and all—you never saw anything like it. You really ought to go out to the end and have a look,' he advised, jerking his head in the direction of the headland.

But before Martin had a chance to go anywhere there was a tap on the window of the trailer behind him, and he looked round to see his mother beckoning to him to come across. She met him in the doorway with the water can in her hand.

'You might fill this,' she said. 'And would you call at the farm for an extra pint of milk, or a quart if they can spare it. I'll never get Linda to eat her breakfast without milk for her corn flakes. And put on your mac, for goodness' sake!'

By the time Martin returned from the farm the water was running off his mackintosh in rivulets, and his mother had to hang it over the sink to save the floor from further wetting. His hopes of seeing the swollen estuary began to fade.

'I'm very sorry, dear,' said his mother when he suggested it. 'But we've just got to be sensible about this business of wet clothes, since I've absolutely no means of drying anything in here, as you can see.'

Then sensing his disappointment she added hopefully:

'Anyway, it surely can't go on like this all day. It'll probably be a lovely afternoon. In the meantime let's make the best of a bad morning and cook up something really special for lunch. How would that be?'

'Oh, could you make us that gorgeous pudding we had at Auntie Mary's?' begged Linda. 'You did write it down in your diary, didn't you?'

'Yes, I wrote it down. But I wonder if I've got all the ingredients for it here. Pass me my bag, will you? Now then, let's see. Yes, I've got eggs all right, and a tin of condensed milk—how lucky it doesn't need fresh milk! Raisins, yes, I've a packet of those. Well, I seem to have everything here as it happens. So now if you two will stone the raisins, I'll get ahead with the rest.'

Martin and Linda sat side by side on the long seat with the bowl of raisins between them, while their mother worked at the cluttered little table. And somehow or other, what with the exciting smells, and occasional tastes of this and that, it turned into quite a good morning after all.

And the meal, when ready, proved even better than they expected. Indeed it was so delicious that they were half way through it before anyone even noticed that the rain had stopped at last.

Before long a hazy sun struggled through the clouds and the damp ground began to steam as the water drained away from all but the deepest puddles. Martin's thoughts strayed off once more to the estuary and the creek. But he wasn't free to be off there yet, for while he and Linda washed the dishes their mother sat down to make out a list of things to be bought at the shop.

'You'll need the big basket to carry all this lot,' she advised.

But just as Martin was about to set off there was an interruption. Mrs Palmer splashed across to see how they were getting on, and she and Mrs Roberts were soon exchanging reminiscences of the night.

'Well now, the point is this,' said Mrs Palmer. 'If we're liable to get such rain as this I need a new mackintosh. So John says why don't I take the car and go into town and buy one. He wants to stay here himself to listen to the racing on the radio. So I was wondering if any of you would like to come for the run? We could have tea at the Windmill Café if you like.'

'Oh, how kind of you,' said Mrs Roberts, and Linda broke in excitedly:

'Then I can spend Auntie Mary's birthday money, can't I? And can I wear my new shorts? And will there be chocolate ices at the Windmill Café? And can I have a raspberry drink with two straws?'

'Oh yes—yes—yes, I expect so!' laughed her mother when she could get a word in, then turning to Mrs Palmer she said smiling:

'As you see we'd love to come. How soon will you be starting?'

'Oh, no special hurry. Half an hour suit you? I just want to get John's tea ready before I go.'

As she turned away Martin took a deep breath.

'Look, Mum,' he began, 'would you awfully mind if I stayed here while you and Lin go to town? I so badly want to go down and see the creek and the estuary before they're back to normal. Mrs Palmer did say "any of us", so she wouldn't think it rude if I stayed here, would she?'

'Oh, I'm sure she'd understand,' said his mother. 'But I don't like the idea of leaving you here on your own.'

'But Mum, I won't be alone. Mr Palmer's just across there, and there's Rocky's mother and heaps of others.'

'Well, but what about your tea?'

'I can make sandwiches. There's sliced bread and the corned beef and all those tomatoes. And you've put bottles of apple juice on the shopping list, so I'll have one of those for a drink. I'll be fine, Mum, really I will. And if I did happen to want anything I can always go in to Mr Palmer.'

'Well, as long as you're sure you'll be all right.'

At his moment Linda skipped out of the trailer in her new shorts.

'And I've put Ben's coat on him too,' she announced. 'So that's two of us ready.'

'Well, if Martin's staying behind Ben might just as well stay too,' began Mrs Roberts.

Martin's heart sank, but Linda came to his aid unexpectedly.

'Oh, but Mum, Ben must come. I've promised him now and he's all excited. Besides, you did say we could buy him a new collar on holiday, didn't you, and you know the shop people never will believe what a fat neck he's got if they don't measure him for themselves.'

'Oh, very well, if you really want to take him,' said her mother, retreating inside to change.

Half an hour later Ben piled into the back of the car with Linda and Brown Teddy. Her mother got into the front with Mrs Palmer. Martin stood on the step of the trailer to see them start.

'Look after yourself,' said his mother.

'And if you want someone to chat to, go across to my husband, he'd be glad of company. Have tea with him if you like—there's any amount of food,' called Mrs Palmer as she let in the clutch.

They all waved, and Linda held Brown Teddy up to the rear window as the car bumped away over the wet grass and turned into the lane.

CHAPTER 5

MARTIN turned back into the trailer with a sigh of relief. Up to the last minute he had been afraid that something would stop them going and his precious afternoon be spoilt.

He decided he would not waste time returning with the shopping; the basket of groceries could quite well be dumped in the old boat with his picnic—he intended to eat there anyway when he had done his exploring.

He was accustomed to making sandwiches, and his meal was soon stuffed into the haversack with his maps and other equipment. He filled his flask with water because he always liked to use it, although it didn't really hold as much as he liked to drink, and he knew he would be glad of the apple juice as well. Then, slinging the haversack over his shoulder, he picked up the basket and went out with the shopping list in his hand.

There was no one about as he crossed the field. Many of the cars were already away, their owners making the most of the sunshine after the morning's rain, whilst the sound of several radios indicated that the few who remained in the camp were preparing to spend a lazy afternoon.

He had just turned into the lane on his way to the shop when he was surprised by the sound of a car. A moment later the Palmers' blue saloon swung into sight and drew up beside him.

'Now what?' he muttered to himself as first his mother, then Linda and Ben got out. He saw that Linda was in tears.

'She's been car-sick,' explained his mother. 'It's my fault of course. I completely forgot to give her a travel pill.'

But even while she spoke the fresh air was reviving the little girl. Martin noticed that his mother was the one who looked pale and tired, and he suspected that she probably had a headache after the broken night. Suddenly he was determined that she should not miss the drive which he knew would do her good.

'Look, Mum, I'll take care of Linda,' he said quickly. 'She can come down to the creek with me while you go to town.'

'Oh no, dear, it's sweet of you to suggest it, but I couldn't leave her like that,' said his mother.

'Oh, but Mummy, you can, I don't feel a bit sick now,' cried Linda, hopping up and down in her anxiety not to miss this chance of exploring with Martin. Her pink cheeks were proof that there was nothing the matter with her now.

Mrs Palmer leant across the steering wheel and said persuasively:

'Oh, do come; you look as though you really need a break after that sleepless night. And as I said, they can go in to John.'

'It's awfully sweet of you, but I really couldn't leave them here alone,' said Mrs Roberts.

45

'But Mum, why ever not?' said Martin. 'Linda often goes to the shop with me, and she went to the creek with me yesterday, so what's the difference if she does the same thing now?'

'I suppose there isn't any difference really, but I'd just feel better if I was here, that's all.'

'Well, we can be here by the time they get back,' Mrs Palmer pointed out. 'We needn't wait for tea, just go straight in and out if you'd rather. By the time Martin's persuaded dear slow old Mrs Williams to sell him all that great list of groceries, and been down to look at the creek, we should easily be back ourselves. After all, it's not much more than nine miles in any case.'

'And I'll take terrific care of her, really I will,' promised Martin.

'And I'll do everything he tells me,' said Linda.

'We'll be absolutely fine, honestly we will,' said Martin, opening the near-side door invitingly.

'Tell John to open the tin of chocolate biscuits for your tea if I'm not back,' called Mrs Palmer as she started up the engine.

Within a few minutes the car had backed out of sight down the lane and they heard the sound of its horn as it turned into the road at the bottom.

Martin turned once more towards the shop, stifling a sigh as he looked down at his companions—a little girl hugging a teddy bear and a fat black dachshund in a coat. What possible chance was there of having an adventurous afternoon with such a party?

There were no other customers in the shop, but old Mrs Williams was even slower than usual, and it was a long time before everything was stowed in the basket. It proved to be a heavy load, and if he had not been impatient at the thought of another delay, Martin might have returned to put the basket in the trailer after all. But as it was he was determined not to waste any more time, and calling to Linda he set off towards the woods.

Despite his coat Ben made no fuss today, plodding manfully down through the woods without a whimper. Linda skipped along behind him, humming to herself. Martin's spirits began to lift.

As they neared the bottom of the hill he became aware of a curious roaring sound that had not been noticeable before. When they reached the edge of the trees they stopped in amazement.

'It doesn't look like the same place even,' said Linda at last.

She was right. Instead of yesterday's glinting river, a tumbling brown torrent now roared between the wooded slopes, tearing at the banks with such ferocity that clods of earth, and even bushes and sapling trees, were torn away, to be swept downstream in a churning welter of dirty yellow foam.

Linda shifted Brown Teddy and reached for Martin's hand.

'Yes, it looks a bit scary, doesn't it?' he agreed, giving her fingers a reassuring squeeze.

It sounded terrifying too, for under the steady rush of water they could hear the grind and bump of tumbled boulders rolling along the bed of the river.

'I wouldn't want to live in the witch's house now,' said Linda, staring across to where the swirling waters swept against the buttressed wall.

'Let's go along to the end anyway,' suggested Martin. 'I

47

want to see the estuary. Rocky says the river has altered its course out there.'

The seaweed-coated rocks had vanished under the racing waters, which now surged through the exposed roots of the riverside trees. Martin drew Linda well back from the edge, and called sharply to Ben to keep to heel as they made their way along to the promontory.

Oddly enough the main estuary was not as turbulent as the creek, since the wider river had more space in which to spread itself. Nevertheless it was an awesome sight, and they stood gazing on it in silence for several minutes.

'Look at all those trees and branches floating down,' whispered Linda. 'Oh, Martin, I don't like it—it looks frightening.'

48

'Come on, let's look at the boathouse, that won't be frightening,' he said cheerfully.

But even the cove was changed today, and they found it reduced to no more than a narrow strip of rock and shingle. Martin moved across to the boathouse, which now stood within a couple of feet of the water. He opened the door and propped it back with a stone.

'The boat's all right anyway,' he said thankfully, dumping his heavy basket in the bows. 'These things will be dryer here in the boat than up there on the wet grass.'

Turning away from the boathouse Linda took a step towards her tree-root cave. But Martin put a restraining hand on her shoulder and held her back.

'Better not go in there today,' he advised. 'We can't tell how much higher the river may rise, and you wouldn't want to be trapped in there among those roots if the water did start trickling through them, would you?'

Linda needed no second warning, and scrambled hastily up to join him on the safety of the bank above. Here she stood with Brown Teddy clasped against her chest, staring across at the old house. Martin laughed down on her and said teasingly:

'That house seems to have cast a spell over you all right! What d'you expect to see there anyway? They aren't really witches, remember.'

But at this moment his attention was caught by Ben, who had wandered down to nose about the tree-root cave on his own. Jumping down the bank Martin caught him by his coat and hauled him up on to the grass beside Linda.

'You'll be safer up here, old fellow,' he said, climbing up himself. Then turning to Linda he remarked:

'The water is still rising. See? It's much nearer to your tree-root cave already, so it's just as well you didn't crawl in there.'

But Linda had eyes for nothing except the house across the water. The place had a deserted air today; the windows were shut and nobody moved in the garden, despite the fact that the river had crept up the bank until it was almost on a level with the narrow lawn. Her eyes turned to the pear tree and she murmured to herself:

'You'd think she'd have to come out to see how her tree looks with its feet in the water, wouldn't you?'

But even as she watched a large section of the garden bank collapsed and crumbled into the river, leaving the pear tree undermined and tottering.

'Oh, the poor tree!' she cried on such a note of distress that Martin's own attention was caught, and he looked up just in time to see the laden tree heel over and fall with terrifying slowness into the river. There it lay, with its uptorn roots on the garden bank, its branches partially submerged in the swirling water. To his surprise it did not immediately float away; evidently a root or two still held it back, resisting the pull of the current. He was just about to turn away when Linda cried out:

'Ah, here she comes down the road!'

He looked to where she was pointing and saw the girl running down the lane towards the house, her hair flying behind her as she ran. She rushed in through the garden gate and made straight for the lawn, where she pulled up short in astonishment. But after no more than a momentary hesitation she darted across to the fallen tree and jumped up on the trunk, steadying herself with a hand on the sprawling roots.

50

'What a stupid thing to do! That tree might easily roll over, or even float away,' exclaimed Martin in a horrified tone.

The girl could now be seen testing the steadiness of the tree, shifting her weight from foot to foot, making sure that it was firm enough to bear her. Then, apparently satisfied, she began to slither down the tilted trunk towards the spot where the water swirled amongst the branches. Reaching forward she caught hold of the stoutest of these branches where it curved up out of the water, and swung herself astride it.

'She must be absolutely mad!' exploded Martin furiously.

'She seems to be looking for something,' said Linda as the girl leant from her perch to thrust her arm amongst the leaves.

'She's no business to go out there anyway, it's much too dangerous,' said Martin, and cupping his hands around his mouth he yelled at the top of his voice:

'Go back! Go back!'

But it was clear that the girl heard nothing above the noise of the water, even when Ben joined in with a volley of excited barking. But it was, in any case, too late for warnings now. The added weight and sudden movement had loosened the remaining roots from their hold on the bank above, leaving the tree at the mercy of the current, which immediately began to draw it away from the shore. As the whole cumbersome mass of leaves and branches swung slowly round and started to drift out into midstream they saw the girl straighten suddenly and look wildly back towards the garden, as though only just aware of what was happening. But the widening gap was already too broad for her to jump.

For one paralysed moment Martin stood watching in horrified fascination. Then in a flash he came to his senses.

'The boat!' he gasped. 'If only I can drag it out by myself!'

There was no need to drag it out, however, for when he ran down the bank he discovered that the cove was now completely under water and the boathouse surrounded. He splashed round to the open doorway to find the floor awash inside and the boat already afloat. It was easy enough to move it now, and it took him no more than a moment to float it out into the open.

Fortunately the water in the cove itself was calm, the main force of the current being confined to the centre of the river. So, although his feet slipped as he stumbled over underwater rocks, he was able to wade out to the end of the promontory without too much difficulty, towing the boat to the foot of the sentinel pine.

Looking up he saw that the floating tree was already nearer, drifting obliquely across the river towards the corner on which he stood. In a few minutes' time it would arrive in the calm water under the promontory, where the boat should be able to reach it without getting into the current at all. This was a comforting thought, since the boat contained no oars.

When he thought the girl could hear him he shouted again:
'Hang on. I'm coming to take you off in a boat.'

She raised her head for a moment and turned a white face in his direction. He could see that she was very frightened, and called again, reassuringly:

'Won't be long now. It's going to be all right.'

He flung himself into the boat, and, holding it steady against the roots, waited for the moment when the tree should float within reach.

'Be ready to get into the boat pretty quickly,' he shouted. 'We'll need to get ourselves clear of the tree before it's carried around the corner into the main estuary.'

He was tensely awaiting the exact moment to push off into deep water when the boat tilted suddenly, and half turning he was horrified to see Linda lowering herself into the stern from the bank above.

'Oh, Linda, go back!' he stormed in sudden fury.

'I'm coming with you. I won't stay here by myself, I'm frightened,' she wailed, starting to sob with fright.

There was no time to put her ashore again, no time to be angry even. The floating tree had almost reached them, and Martin, timing it carefully, shoved the boat out from the bank with a powerful thrust that carried it several yards offshore, where it lay directly in the path of the oncoming tree.

He was so intent on what lay ahead that he did not notice a splash behind as Ben plunged from the bank and swam desperately after the boat. Linda saw him, however, and it was she who seized him by his saturated coat and heaved him scrabbling over the stern and into her lap.

54

'Now hush,' she cautioned, gripping him tightly against her so that he could not shake himself and so warn Martin of his presence.

The tree was now within a few yards of them. Martin saw the frightened eyes of the girl fixed on him.

'Hold on tight,' he directed her, 'and when we touch I'll hang on to one of the branches while you get into the boat as quickly as ever you can. The minute you're in I'll push off again; one good strong shove should get us back—that was all it took to bring us out.'

Next minute the tree was upon them, its spreading branches scooping the boat into a leafy embrace.

'Duck down, Linda, shut your eyes, and whatever you do hang on for all you're worth!' he shouted, startled by the force with which the tree bore down on them, smothering them in leaves and snapping twigs, while loosened pears thudded on to the floorboards at their feet.

'Catch hold of one of the branches, Lin,' he ordered, clinging to one himself. 'We mustn't let the boat drift away from the tree before she's in, whatever happens.'

The girl, meanwhile, was doing her best to wriggle along her bough towards the boat, which lay like a gigantic wooden nest amongst the encircling branches. But half way along the bough she paused to say hesitantly:

'Don't you think I'd better stay here, perhaps? Three of us would make an awfully heavy load in that old boat—it looks pretty leaky as it is.'

Martin glanced down and was dismayed to see how much water had seeped in through the rotten planking.

'But how else can we get you ashore?' he said.

'I don't think that boat could get us as far as the shore,' said the girl above him quietly.

'Oh, but it's hardly any distance; one push brought us out here,' he began, glancing back over his shoulder as he spoke. But he now saw that the cove and promontory had already dropped astern, whilst their extraordinary entanglement of boat and branches had been swept around the corner and was rapidly being carried out into the main estuary.

For the first time Martin felt a prickle of fear. The estuary was a deserted place, bounded by miles of sand dunes and unfrequented beaches. No houses stood along the shore and there would be nobody to see them pass, unless someone from the trailer camp should happen to wander out to the end of the headland. But that was most unlikely, as late in the day as this. He had a momentary vision of being swept helplessly out to sea with no one to see and report where they had gone.

But there was no time to dwell on such thoughts for long. Already the water was swirling around his feet and there was Linda to look after. In his anxiety he didn't even stop to wonder how Ben had got into the boat.

'I wonder if we might all be safer in the branches perhaps,' he said, speaking as calmly as he could. 'Obviously the tree won't sink, but this poor old boat looks as though she might go down at any minute. Anyway, Lin, hang on to that branch with both hands just in case the boat really does go down under us.'

'What about Ben?' quavered Linda. 'He can't hold on to anything.'

'I'm afraid he'll just have to swim if the worst comes to the worst. We'd better get his coat off though; he'll swim more freely without it.'

56

'I'll take it off,' she cried, letting go of her branch immediately.

'Linda!' bawled Martin. 'Didn't you hear me tell you to hang on to that branch with both hands? *Both hands!* That's better. Now don't let go whatever you do. I'll get it off him myself. Here, Benbow, come here. There, that's better, isn't it?'

Despite the speed and strength of the current, the tree floated surprisingly slowly, at times appearing almost stationary in the water.

'Lucky it's a big tree anyway,' remarked the girl. 'At least it doesn't plunge up and down in the water like some I've seen today.'

'It's got gorgeous pears on it, hasn't it?' remarked Linda. 'Some have even fallen into the boat.' Her eyes wandered questioningly to Martin, wondering whether he might suggest her eating one. But Martin's mind was far from thoughts of food.

Linda turned her attention to the girl, noting that she was not in the least like a witch after all.

'Your name's Alex, isn't it?' she said, and when the girl nodded she went on: 'Mine's Linda, and our dog's called Ben and this is Brown Teddy. We used to watch you in the garden with the old witch.' She caught herself up suddenly, remembering how uncomfortable Martin had looked when she mentioned the witch to Janet. But Alex was staring across the water with an anxious look in her eyes. She had far more to worry about than Linda's conversation. Already there were signs of an early twilight, and her thoughts, like Martin's, turned to hopes of rescue.

Linda sighed and returned her attention to the pears. One

57

had rolled under the forward thwart and was bobbing about in the puddle of water collected there. They were beautiful pears, small and smooth and yellow. Her mouth watered longingly.

'We've stopped!' yelled Martin suddenly.

'How can we have?' demanded Alex. 'We're nowhere near the bank.'

'I don't know how, but we have. Look at those sticks floating past us.'

'We certainly do seem to be stuck on something,' admitted Alex slowly. 'I can see a patch of sand down there under the branches. The only thing is, there just *isn't* any land out here in the estuary. I don't understand it.'

'Neither do I,' said Martin, in a voice as bewildered as her own. 'I've looked down on all this from the cliff top several times. I've even made a map of it, so I know there just aren't any islands out here. And yet—and yet—this *is* land, you know. Look, there's sand here, right under the boat, and more over there where the waves are breaking.'

'Yet we're a long way out from the shore,' puzzled Alex, looking round. 'I'd say we're almost in the middle of the channel. It's the queerest thing I've ever known.'

'I say! I've just remembered something!' cried Martin, suddenly recalling Rocky's news of the morning. 'Someone up there in the trailer camp said that the river had altered its course in the storm. He said it looked quite different.'

'Well, of course there always have been odd patches of rough water out here,' mused Alex. 'It used to look as though there might be sand-banks just below the surface. Perhaps one of those has shifted and piled itself up a bit so that it's now become an island. Could it have, I wonder?'

58

'Well, it feels quite firm anyway,' observed Martin, leaning over the side. 'I must say I'd rather have this under our leaky old boat than all that water!'

'Can I get out and feel how firm it is?' asked Linda, sliding to the edge of her seat.

'Certainly not, you stay where you are,' ordered Martin firmly.

'Well then—d'you think—oh, please, could I eat a pear?' she begged.

'Of course, help yourself,' said Alex, smiling absently.

So with a deep, contented sigh Linda sank her teeth into a juicy pear. Ben stood beside her, dribbling quietly as he waited for the core, while the elder two reviewed the situation.

CHAPTER 6

STILL gripping his branch, Martin slid one leg over the edge of
the boat and cautiously tested the sand with his bare foot.

'Feels quite firm, considering it's so wet,' he reported.

Alex lowered herself through the branches until she stood on
the sand beside the boat.

'Perfectly firm,' she agreed.

'Do please hang on to a branch all the same,' he begged.
'I'm so afraid it may be soft in patches.'

'Can I try?' asked Linda.

'No,' said Martin very decidedly.

Ben, on the other hand, waited for no one's permission, and
leapt out of the boat before they could stop him. He landed
heavily, his large paws sinking deeply into the yielding sand.

But after a moment's surprised hesitation he managed to squelch forward, step by step.

'Well, it bears him anyway, and he's heavy enough, goodness knows!' said Martin, smiling for the first time.

'Just look how quickly the boat's drying out,' said Linda. And indeed the puddles had gone, the water draining away through the cracks as easily as it had flowed in.

'How lucky the food didn't get wet,' she added, crawling forward to inspect the basket in the bows. Then noticing a packet of dog biscuits she pounced on it.

'Oh, look, Ben's special favourite kind of biscuits!' she cried delightedly. 'Can I give him some now? It must be ages past his dinner time.'

Ben always seemed to have an extra sense where food was concerned, and although Linda hadn't spoken directly to him he guessed what she was talking about, and came to stand on his hind legs against the side of the boat, clawing the wood with his forepaws and whimpering to be lifted in.

'You wanted to get out a moment ago,' laughed Martin, hoisting him over the side.

Linda opened the bag and took out a handful of biscuits.

'Now wait, Ben, you're not to snatch,' she cautioned, holding out the biscuits one at a time.

'Oh, isn't he sweet!' breathed Alex as the little dog took the biscuits very gently, and then crunched them up with a good deal of noise.

'Now that's enough,' said Martin presently. 'He'll eat the lot if you let him. You can give him a drink though; I've got some water here in my flask. Look, there's an old bailer under the thwart over there; he can use that as a drinking bowl. Don't give him all the water now though,' he warned, handing over the flask. 'He might need more later on.'

'Couldn't we have our own tea now? This island seems a lovely place for a picnic,' suggested Linda.

Martin and Alex looked at each other across her head, very conscious of the fact that they might be forced to remain on the so-called island a good deal longer than they intended. Alex glanced towards the headland, but there was no sign of life, either there or anywhere else along the sandy shore, which was already blurred with approaching twilight.

'Well, I suppose we might as well eat,' agreed Martin. 'This island seems to be getting bigger every minute. I'm sure there's more sand here now than when we landed.'

'Tide's still going out, that's why,' Alex pointed out. 'And I tell you another thing,' she added, after studying the river intently for a while. 'This tree is forming a sort of barrier; its branches are so thick with leaves that they are holding the water back like a dam and actually stopping it from washing over this end of the island at all.'

Martin looked round and saw that she was right; the solid bulk of the tree was dividing the river into two distinct streams which swept by on either side of them, leaving the central ridge of sand high and dry.

'You know we're lucky in another way too,' he observed. 'We've got lots more food than just my sandwiches here; we've got all those things we bought at the shop for Mum.'

'And two bottles of milk as well,' Linda reminded him.

'Yes, better drink those before we start on the apple juice. We don't want any more milk going sour. Not that it looks thundery now,' he went on, his mind turning to the weather lore he had studied as part of his explorer training. 'I don't see any anvil-shaped clouds about, anyway.'

'I'm afraid the only food I've brought is pears, but I've certainly got enough of those!' laughed Alex, waving a hand at the laden branches surrounding them. 'And they ought to be eaten quickly too,' she went on. 'Pears are such tricky things, hard one day and sleepy-soft a few days later, and only really perfect for a short while in between. We've been watching these all the week and they only started getting right yesterday.'

'Then perhaps you'd pick some for us now, while I get out the other things,' said Martin, reaching for his haversack.

Using the middle thwart as a table he spread out the food. In addition to the sandwiches he had brought, he took some buns and biscuits from the shopping basket, also the two pint bottles of milk. Alex added four good-sized pears.

'Why four?' questioned Linda in surprise.

'One for Ben, of course,' explained Alex. 'There's no need for him to be fobbed off with cores if he really likes pears; we've got more here than we'll ever want for ourselves.'

'Better give him the smallest then, or he might be sick,' advised Martin as Linda reached forward to take one. In three gulps Ben's pear was gone, then a sleek black head slid on to Martin's knee and two brown eyes looked up beseechingly.

'No, Ben, you've had all that's good for you, so it's no use cadging from me,' he said. 'On second thoughts, perhaps you'd better run about outside while we have our meal. There, over you go!' With which he lowered the little dog on to the sand outside.

'He's bound to be quite safe out there, isn't he?' he said suddenly, turning to Alex for reassurance. 'I mean, this whole island couldn't go down suddenly under him, could it?'

'Oh, surely not,' said Alex. 'It's getting bigger, not smaller, anyway, and the tide must have at least another hour to ebb. Yes, look over there: there's quite a tide-mark of odds and ends along the edge of the sand, that just shows how much the tide has gone down since we arrived.'

'It's turned into a real little beach on that side,' said Linda. 'Oh, isn't this a wonderful island that we've found! Have we got any cups? I'm thirsty.'

There weren't any cups, so they had to drink out of the bottles of milk in turns, taking short drinks at the start so as to share the creamy top quite fairly.

When they had finished Linda turned to Martin.

'Can I go and explore the island now?' she begged.

'Surely you can see all you want from here?' he said discouragingly. He felt horribly responsible for Linda.

'Oh, Martin, there's lots I can't see from here. I want to go right inside the tree where it's like a little secret house among the branches. Please, Martin.'

'I'll go with her,' put in Alex quickly. 'I promise to take good care of her. And actually I want to see every bit of the island too while we're here.'

At any other time Martin would have been the first to wish to explore the island himself, working out its compass points and area, and making a detailed sketch map. But now he was weighed down with anxious responsibility. There was still no sign of life on shore, and it was rapidly growing dark. His heart turned over when he thought of his mother returning to the empty trailer.

He little guessed that his mother's plans had also been upset by the storm. She and Mrs Palmer got through their shopping quickly and were on their way home when the car was halted by a policeman.

'Road closed!' he informed them cheerfully. 'The storm has turned the river into a proper torrent and it's just swept part of the bridge away.'

'But we came over it half an hour ago!' cried Mrs Palmer incredulously.

'Well, I'm afraid you can't go back over it now,' he answered.

'But we've *got* to get back,' cried Mrs Roberts, leaning anxiously across to speak to him. 'If we leave the car here can we get across on foot?'

The man shook his head decidedly.

'Not a hope,' he replied. 'And the ferry can't make it either of course, with the river running like this. So if you want to get across this evening you'll have to go way up round by the mountain road to the new bridge, I'm afraid.'

'The mountain road!' Mrs Palmer was aghast. 'But it'll take us hours and hours that way!'

'Sorry, ma'am, but that's the way it is,' he said, moving back to stop another car.

'We must look for a telephone. I must call and make sure the children are all right,' said Mrs Roberts.

'There isn't a phone in the camp,' Mrs Palmer reminded her. 'But John will take care of them. Thank goodness I told them to go to him! My word, though, we'll be driving half the night by the look of this map; it's absolutely miles. Well, I'd better turn the car and get moving right away.'

By a strange chance old Mrs Challenor was also caught on the wrong side of the wrecked bridge. She had crossed it on her way to the hospital earlier in the day, and when it was time for

65

her to return the bridge was no longer there. The friends with whom she had had tea decided that the mountain road would be altogether too much for the old lady to face so late in the day, even in a taxi, so they persuaded her to spend the night with them.

'It's been a long and tiring day for you,' they pointed out, 'and Alex couldn't be in better hands. You told her to wait at the Simpsons' cottage until you called for her anyway, so when you don't turn up they'll obviously keep her there and give her a bed, just as they did on the night of your daughter's operation. They've probably heard about the bridge by this time in any case, so they won't be expecting you back.'

As the colour drained out of the day the last of the light lingered about the new little island out in the estuary, touching it with an afterglow of gold, until its pears hung like dim gold lamps above the golden sand. The tranquil beauty entered into Martin's heart, and his worries gradually faded before the sounds of talk and laughter, as the other two scrambled amongst the branches of the tree. They had discovered many secluded corners where the sandy floor was encircled and roofed with leafy branches.

Linda called excitedly:

'Martin! You must come in here and see it; it's exactly like a little house with heaps and heaps of rooms, all with smooth sandy floors and leafy walls, and pears hanging from the ceilings ready for the next meal.'

'It really does make an exciting place,' added Alex. 'Somehow it doesn't seem like my same old tree any more, it's so full of secret corners now. You really ought to come in here and see it for yourself.'

Ben was busily snuffling from room to leafy room, squeezing under low boughs and pushing his way through walls of leaves, having quite forgotten that he was a town dog who expected to be helped over awkward places.

'This is the drawing-room,' explained Linda, as Martin lowered himself through the branches. 'And this is the pantry because it's got the most pears hanging in it. And this tiny one is the laundry because the sand is still wet in here—and look, Martin, you must look!' she pleaded, catching his hand to hold his interest. 'It really is a very good laundry because if I dig a

hole like this, then it fills up quite soon like a little basin with a secret tap. Look, isn't that good? And we've even got a drying-rack up here, where we've hung Ben's coat to dry; doesn't it look nice?'

'And I've found my old study up here, almost like it used to be, only the other way round,' called Alex from the branches over their heads.

When every corner of the tree house had been explored and explained they went back to the boat, which had now dried out sufficiently to allow them to sit on the floorboards with their backs against the curving hull as they discussed the situation.

'They'll surely come and look for us soon,' said Martin. 'So we'd better just wait here till they arrive. Not that we can do anything else of course; this boat's obviously too leaky to take us as far as the shore, even if we had any oars.'

'Why should we want to go anywhere else? It's so lovely here on our island,' said Linda contentedly. 'Brown Teddy loves it here, and you can see that Ben does too, he's so waggy. Here, Benbow, come and lie by me, there's a good boy.'

'Will your people be worrying about you?' asked Martin, turning to Alex.

'Well, no, because Mrs Challenor thinks I'm with the Simpsons; she saw me get into the bus to go there. Luckily they aren't on the phone themselves, so they said I could just go up there whenever I wanted to, while Aunt Joan's in hospital. So they wouldn't have known I was coming today until I got there anyway.'

'Well, I only hope our mother hasn't got back quite yet,' said Martin anxiously. 'But, oh dear, she'll be just about frantic when she does get back, I'm afraid.'

'But there are heaps of people up there in the camp; someone is sure to help her when she tells them you aren't back.'

'Well yes, there's Mr Palmer, he might help, I suppose. Only how will they know which way we went? There wasn't anyone about when we started out.'

'Oh, I dare say somebody's spotted this island by now. They might even phone for the lifeboat,' said Alex calmly.

'The lifeboat? For us? Might they really?' gasped Martin, realizing that this was turning into a very big adventure indeed. He began to feel more hopeful about his mother.

'What a good thing you got all those groceries; they'll keep us going for ages,' said Alex. 'That sliced bread will be a big help, and the potato crisps and the tin of corned beef—oh, but of course we haven't got a tin-opener.'

'*I* have. There's one on the knife Daddy sent me from Singapore,' said Martin, pulling the splendid weapon from his pocket and opening its numerous gadgets for her to see.

'Oh, I say, how marvellous! I never saw one with so many bits and pieces,' she said admiringly.

'Daddy got it because Martin's going to be an explorer,' Linda explained. 'I'm going to be a mummy when I grow up. Janet says you're a writer.'

'That's what I'd *like* to be,' corrected Alex, darting an embarrassed glance at Martin, dreading his possible scorn. 'But I haven't had anything published yet of course. I don't suppose I ever will really. Most people say I won't anyway.'

'Janet says your writing's very good,' observed Linda.

'What sort of things do you write?' inquired Martin. At the sight of their friendly interest Alex relaxed and smiled.

'Oh, stories mostly. But it's fun describing real things too.

like this adventure. You see I easily might want to put this sort of thing into a book one day.'

'Would we be in the book?' demanded Linda, her blue eyes very wide.

'You might be,' said Alex. 'I was writing all about the flood this morning, sitting up there in the pear tree. It used to be my secret study for writing in, but I don't suppose I'll ever use it again now,' and she glanced sadly up at the branch on which she had spent so many happy hours.

'You ought to climb up there now and write something very special about us all on the island,' said Linda. 'Only you haven't got anything to write with.'

'Ah, but I have! I left my writing things up there in the tree in my haversack when Mrs Challenor called me in this morning to tell me about going to the Simpsons'. I never remembered them again till I was actually in the bus. Luckily I'd only gone a little way, so I got out at the next stop and ran home by a short cut to collect them. I meant to catch the next bus up of course.'

'We saw you running down the lane,' said Linda. Then recalling the scene she went on: 'Was that why you got on the fallen tree, to look for your haversack?'

When Alex nodded the small girl turned triumphantly to her brother.

'There you are!' she cried. 'I said she was looking for something, didn't I? So she wasn't so silly as you thought, she couldn't leave her writing things behind, could she?'

'But surely the haversack wasn't still there on the branch, and still dry?' said Martin, remembering the fallen tree lying partially submerged in the river.

'Well, the outside had got a bit wet,' she confessed. 'But the inside was quite all right. So now I really will be able to make it into an exciting story! And I'll be able to write it on the spot, which will make it so much more real. Only it's getting too dark to write anything now of course. I wonder what time it is.'

'Pretty late, I should imagine,' said Martin. 'Funny how you can't see a single shore light anywhere from here.'

'Well, there aren't any houses along this part of the estuary,' Alex reminded him. 'But at least there is a lighthouse—see it way out there where the estuary joins the sea?'

'Doesn't it have a nice friendly look, the way it winks at us?' murmured Linda. She was beginning to grow sleepy, and before long her head dropped against Martin's arm and she closed her eyes.

The other two lapsed into a long silence as they listened to the steady ripple of the current flowing past on either side of their narrow ridge of sand.

Night seemed to fall on them suddenly, a deep velvety night, with the sky ablaze with stars.

'How close they seem,' murmured Alex. 'It makes you feel sort of safe just to see them there, doesn't it?'

'Yes,' agreed Martin. 'Somehow one always feels better with stars. Explorers like them specially of course, because they help them to know where they are.'

Ben shifted his position, edging up closer to Linda. Disturbed, she opened her eyes for an instant.

'Oh stars—stars . . .' she whispered sleepily, closing her eyes again.

Martin's own eyes turned to the shadowy outline of the pear

tree, and for the first time he noticed just how deeply the boat had been driven into the tangle of its branches when they grounded.

'D'you know something?' he mused, speaking more to himself than to Alex. 'I reckon we'll be all right even if the water does come over the island again at high tide. We know this tree will float whatever happens, and I don't believe the boat could possibly sink now either; it's got so mixed up with the tree that I'm pretty sure the branches would hold it up.'

'Like a swan's nest floating on a raft of matted reeds,' murmured Alex drowsily. It was a comforting thought with which to close their eyes, and soon, lulled by the rustle of the encircling river, they were as deeply asleep as Linda and Ben.

As the night wore on the wind dropped and a soft white mist began to form, drifting over the river and dimming the watchful stars.

CHAPTER 7

AT INTERVALS throughout the night the island was filled with
the sound of wings and fluting calls, as wave after wave of
migrating birds swept over, calling to one another as they
headed towards the sea.

Martin opened his eyes in the darkness and heard Alex stir
in the bow.

'Must be the sandpipers and the rest of them starting off,'
she murmured sleepily.

'And the martins too,' he added, remembering the twittering
group lining the telegraph wires above the ferry cottage.
Closing his eyes again he fancied he could hear those twitterings
now, amongst the liquid calls of the larger birds.

When next he opened his eyes it was daylight. The first
thing he saw was a golden pear hanging on a branch above his
head. The sight of it brought memories of the previous evening

flooding back. He sat up abruptly and looked about him. First he glanced at his companions. On one side of him Alex lay curled in the bow with her head on her haversack. On the other side Linda had the sleeping Ben as a pillow.

He now looked beyond the boat. He saw at once that their island had grown larger during the night. The pear tree branches had caught up so much drifting wreckage that it had piled into a considerable breakwater, around which the river divided into two ever deepening channels, running on either side of the protected spit of sand.

Although there was still plenty of water coming down it was no longer muddy, and very little now floated on its surface. However, not much of the surface could be seen this morning, since a dense mist lay over the water, enclosing the sandy island in cloudy whiteness. Above the mist the sun was shining, its brightness penetrating the haze and bathing the island in a soft, unearthly light which lent it a strange air of unreality.

Ben raised his head and yawned loudly, waking Linda. She sat up, blinking in momentary bewilderment. Then a happy smile spread over her face.

'Oh, we're still on our lovely island!' she cried. 'So it wasn't a dream after all. Although', she added, staring round on the mist-enchanted scene, 'it looks like a dream place this morning, doesn't it? Can I get up now? Or are we up?'

Martin nodded absently, his mind already busy with the problems of the day.

'Well, we can't clean our teeth today anyway,' she remarked with satisfaction. 'And isn't it easy, not having to dress? Just like being a dog, only dogs shake themselves, of course. Come on, Benbow, let's go for a walk on our island, shall we?'

'Careful, for goodness' sake,' warned Martin automatically, as Linda climbed out of the boat, dragging Ben after her.

'Oh, it's as firm as firm this morning,' she assured him, stamping her feet on the sand to prove her words. 'And look over there, we've got an even better beach on our island now, with shells and a proper high-tide mark and everything. Ben and me are going to be the very first two to walk on it ever.'

When Alex woke and saw the mist she jumped up and looked about her anxiously.

'I wonder how we'll get away from here now with this fog,' she said in a worried tone. 'Nobody will be able to see where we are.'

'Oh, I expect it will clear as the day goes on,' Martin assured her, trying to feel as confident as he sounded. 'Anyway we'll be safe enough here—this tree makes a marvellous break-water; because of it our sand's quite dry this morning, and wonderfully firm. And thanks to all that shopping I did we've plenty of food and quite a lot of drink.'

'And the pears as well—they'll help to quench our thirst a bit and eke out the drink, won't they?' added Alex. She was feeling calmer already under Martin's leadership.

'They certainly will. But I think it would be a good plan to review the store situation now,' said Martin. He was suddenly beginning to enjoy himself, realizing that after all his doubts and worries this had turned into a full-scale expedition, every bit as exciting as anything he had ever planned or imagined. But he was also very well aware that real-life expeditions need very careful organization, and he was determined to make this one a success. He pulled the heavy shopping-basket towards him and began to take out the contents, arranging everything methodically in the bows of the boat.

'Shall I get breakfast ready while you sort out the stores?' suggested Alex, wiping the stern thwart clear of sand with her sleeve. 'If you'll just pass me what we can have for breakfast I'll lay it out here on the seat.'

'Good idea,' said Martin. 'Well, here's the bread for a start; we'd better use up the perishable goods first and keep the tins for later on. And here's a jar of jam and a bottle of apple juice. But we'll have to be careful with the drinks—there's no knowing how long they may have to last us.'

Alex prized the lid off the jam with a twig from the pear tree.

'Good thing it's raspberry,' she observed. 'I think that's the best jam to have without butter, don't you? I wish I'd a knife to spread it with, though.'

Martin considered his penknife, but as it was the only tool of any kind on the island he dared not risk clogging its blade with jam. He was still wondering what else they could use when Linda skipped up with her hands full of treasures from the tide-line.

'Just look what I found on our beach,' she cried. 'Washed-up flowers and a bottle and a rubber glove and this funny long shell.'

'Ah, a razor shell, exactly what I need for spreading this jam,' said Alex, holding out her hand.

Linda stepped back a pace.

'Oh, but I wanted to keep it,' she objected. 'It'll be horrid all sticky with jam.'

Martin swung round impatiently.

'Now look here, Lin,' he said seriously, 'this isn't just a game, you know, we aren't playing at desert islands now. This is a *real* desert island, and we are really stranded on it, and

76

we've all got to give what help we can until we're rescued. Understand?'

Linda nodded solemnly, her eyes fixed on his face.

'This is an awfully big adventure we're having, isn't it?' she said.

'Yes, a much bigger adventure than most little girls of six are ever likely to have in their whole lives. So for goodness' sake

try to behave like a real-life castaway, since you are lucky enough to be one.'

'I bet Rocky hasn't never had such a big adventure as this,' she remarked, handing over her razor shell. Alex plunged it into the jam and started to spread slices of bread which she put on the seat.

'I think we could spare a tin of sardines as well,' decided Martin. 'There are two tins here, and one of meat, so we're quite well off.'

'I love sardines,' said Linda, watching Alex fit the key in the tin and roll back the lid. This done, she wiped the razor shell on a scrap of bread, and using it as a spoon, scooped the sardines out of the tin and divided them equally on to three slices of bread.

'Three each and one over,' breathed Linda, hanging over the edge of the boat to watch. 'Oh, please, could Ben have the extra one? He simply adores sardines.'

'Well, just let me pour some of the oil on our bread first,' said Alex, tipping up the tin. When she had done she handed it over.

'There you are,' she said. 'And here's a bit of bread to mop up the rest of the oil for him, pity to waste any of it.'

Linda wiped out the tin very thoroughly, dropping the oily pieces of bread into the bailer with the one sardine before putting it down for Ben.

'Shall I throw the tin into the river, Martin?' she asked. 'I'm so afraid Ben might get hold of it and cut his mouth like he did with a meat tin once.'

'O.K. But fill it with sand first to make sure it sinks, and throw it far out where the water's deep,' he directed.

'Breakfast's ready!' called Alex.

'Can I take mine into the pear tree dining-room?' begged Linda.

'If you like. But you'll have to come back here when you want your drink, as we'll all have to share the bottle,' Martin reminded her.

'I don't mind,' she assured him, and gathering up her share of the food she crawled into the depths of the tree.

Dry bread, sardines and raspberry jam, washed down with apple juice, may sound a peculiar breakfast to you, but the three island castaways could never remember enjoying a meal so much.

'And pears to finish with,' said Alex. 'Can you pick us some from the pantry while you're in there, Linda? Choose the yellowest ones you can find. And one for Ben, remember.'

'But it seems so wasteful to give him a whole one every time,' objected Martin. 'He really scarcely tastes them, you know.'

'I know, but he might just as well have them—there's no point in saving them now,' Alex reminded him. 'After all, this poor old tree can't live very long, I'm afraid, stranded out here on the sand with no proper earth for its roots.'

'Oh, will it really die?' cried Linda in distress. 'It's such a nice tree, and it makes such a good house for our island.'

Nobody answered, so she turned her attention to her pear and soon forgot everything else in the delight of its juiciness. The other two ate theirs in the boat, while Ben gulped his down on the sand outside, almost choking in his excitement.

'Funny not to have anything to wash up but a razor shell!' laughed Alex when they had finished.

'Oh, can I wash it up, please?' cried Linda, reaching out through a leafy window to take it.

'There, isn't it lovely and clean?' she said when she brought it back. 'I'll put it down here in the shopping-basket, shall I?'

Then, wiping her hands on her shorts, she turned to Martin.

'What are we going to do now?' she asked.

'You must amuse yourself. I've got things to attend to,' he replied.

'So've I got things to attend to too,' said Linda grandly. 'I'm going to make a garden.'

'A garden? But we haven't got any flowers,' objected Alex, looking at her in surprise.

'Oh, but we have, there's lots of flowers washed up on our beach. I'll make them into a garden easily. You'll see,' said Linda, and picking Brown Teddy out of the boat she ran off with Ben at her heels.

Martin straightened up and turned in the direction of the shore, which was still completely blanketed in mist.

'No chance of anyone spotting us yet awhile, not till this mist clears anyway,' he remarked. 'Do you get these mists here often?'

'Well, I'm only here in the holidays so I'm not quite sure,' said Alex. 'Anyway, nothing is quite the same as usual now in any case, because this island isn't usually here, remember.'

After a moment's silence she went on:

'That reminds me. I'd better get all this adventure written down now at once, whilst it's fresh in my mind.'

She pulled her haversack towards her and undid the buckles and took out a hard-covered exercise book and a ball-point pen. Then glancing up at the pear tree she remarked:

'I always loved writing in this old tree, so I may as well climb up and write there now. I suppose this will be the last thing I'll ever write in my pear-tree study—how I wish it could turn out to be the best thing I've ever written!'

Martin had been making his own plans meanwhile, and now he also reached for his haversack and took out his compass, a steel tape measure, notebook and pencil.

'Whatever are you going to do with all those?' asked Alex, leaning down from her perch in the tree.

'Make a sketch map of the island,' he replied briefly.

'A map—oh, Martin, how simply thrilling! D'you know how to make one properly? Oh, just think of mapping a perfectly new island, one that's never been explored or charted before, because it's never been in the world till now! Well, by the time you've made a map of it, and I've written an account of the whole exploration, it'll be a pretty important place, won't it? What are we going to call it, by the way? Explorers always give names to islands when they discover them.'

'They often give them their own names,' began Martin slowly.

'Oh, but that's dull,' she said. 'I like names like Easter Island or Christmas Island. Only it isn't any special season now of course. I know, how about calling it September Island?'

Martin considered this before replying.

'Yes,' he said at last. 'That's a good name, a very good name, I think.'

Alex flicked open her notebook and wrote 'THE DIS-COVERY OF SEPTEMBER ISLAND' in capital letters across the top of the page.

'Oh, it looks simply marvellous in print!' she breathed. Then, hunching over the book on her knee, she began to write in earnest.

81

CHAPTER 8

MARTIN went to work on his map methodically. First he considered the scale. The island was long and narrow, so narrow that he could toss a stone across it from shore to shore. He judged it to be about forty yards long, but when he paced it out he found it to be nearer fifty. He would measure it properly later, of course, but this gave him a rough idea to work on. Since his notebook was less than seven inches long the map could only be a small one. He decided that his scale should be one inch to ten yards.

Next he checked the compass points. He knew from the direction of the river that the island must lie roughly north and south, so he chose its longest stretch as a base line. He then laid his notebook on the ground, parallel with this line, and placing the compass on the open page, drew an arrow in line with the compass needle pointing north. His father had explained that a compass only gives magnetic north, and had shown him how to find the magnetic variation. So he was now able to cross the arrow with a second line which indicated true north. He marked this line NS.

The next part of the job took a lot of time and patience, since it entailed driving the longest sticks he could find into the ground, taking their compass bearings and measuring the distances between them. It was a slow business, but he eventually got the outline of the island drawn satisfactorily. Now he came to the best part of the job, and found himself wishing there were more exciting details to fill in. However, he remembered that the maps in *Treasure Island* and some other favourite books hadn't had such a lot of details either. Perhaps in a way that made the few entries all the more important.

To begin with there was the pear tree. It was not, of course, actually growing on the island, nevertheless it was very much alive, and in a sense it almost gave the island being. For if the powerful spread of its protecting boughs had not divided the river around their narrow spit of sand, the island itself might no longer be in existence.

Next he noted the position of the boat. He decided to mark it as a wreck since it was unlikely that it would ever be fit to sail again—and anyway a wreck looked most exciting! Then, picking out the highest points on the almost flat little island, he sketched them in as sandhills, determined to make use of the nice little pattern of lines and dots that map-makers used for sandhills. Nor could he resist entering the dampest bit of the island as marsh, since that enabled him to put in another symbol he liked.

This done, he got up and prowled about the island in search

of any other features that might help to make his map more interesting.

The curve of the island which Linda described as a beach did, in fact, form a shallow bay which gave the island a very distinctive shape. He was studying this when a welcoming bark from Ben drew his attention to Linda herself, squatting at the lower end of this bay. He had noticed her there while pacing out the island, and he now went across to see what she was doing.

'Why, Lin, you really have made a garden!' he exclaimed, staring down in astonishment on the colourful patch she had planted, and edged with shells and pebbles.

'I found lots of flowers washed up when I looked, there was even some tangled up in the branches of the pear tree,' she told him, wiping her sandy hands on her shirt and sitting back on her heels to hear what he thought of her work.

There were not only flowers in Linda's garden, there were also small uprooted saplings and a fine little gorse bush bright with yellow bloom. At one side stood a forest of feathers, stuck into the sand like trees. Most of these were fairly large, their colours ranging from brown and buff to grey. But scattered amongst them, like flowers in the dusky forest, were some that were small and white. Martin recalled the snowy breasts of the birds on the telegraph wire, and wondered.

'Where did you find all these feathers, Lin?' he questioned.

'Oh, they were scattered all over the sand,' she answered, waving her hand in the direction of the bay. 'There were hundreds of bird footprints too, running criss-cross all over the beach.'

Martin remembered the bird calls in the darkness, and wondered how many of the night travellers had chosen this

84

narrow ridge of sand as their final landfall before launching out over the sea. It seemed a tiny starting-point for such a tremendous journey. He wondered whether the birds set out with just such hopes as human explorers know. There had been a yearning note in the wistful cries, and he hoped that at their journey's end they would also find their moment of delight.

Suddenly it occurred to him that some of these birds were martins, and he exclaimed aloud:

'Well, so am I a Martin, so perhaps this island is going to be the starting-point of all *my* travels too!' At the thought his spirits soared as the birds had soared in the darkness.

Linda said nothing, not at all sure what he was talking about. But when he squatted down beside her garden and balanced his notebook on his knee she leant over his shoulder, watching with breathless interest.

'Your garden is going to make all the difference to this bottom bit of my map,' he remarked, getting to work with his pencil.

'Oh, Martin, is that my name what you're writing now?' she cried excitedly, seeing him print 'Linda's Garden' in small, neat letters.

'That's right. I only wish I could list all these flowers as "Island Flora" though,' he said. 'After all, they really are growing here now. Only the worst of it is I don't know their names.'

'I expect Alex will know,' said Linda. 'She seems to know all about things like that, doesn't she?'

'That's an idea,' said Martin. 'Anyway I'll make a heading here in the back of the book, and list them later if she can help me.'

'Oh, Martin, look!' she shouted in sudden excitement. 'We've got a butterfly on our island too, a white one, coming to smell my flowers!' She was almost beside herself with delight that so beautiful a visitor should single out her little garden for special attention.

Martin crouched on the sand behind her, writing 'Island Fauna' beside the 'Island Flora' heading. In this second column he entered the butterfly, merely describing it as 'white'.

'Notice the markings on its wings, Lin, and try to remember them if you can. Then we might be able to find its full name in a butterfly book when we get home.'

86

He glanced at the feathers and sighed regretfully, knowing that he would never be able to list the birds that had alighted on the island overnight, leaving no more than a scattering of feathers, and trails of delicate footprints in the sand as evidence of their visit. They would have to remain a part of the mystery that surrounded this strange little island. As for the flowers, they must wait until Alex was free to name them. But glancing across at her now he saw that she was still scribbling away at a great pace, and knew that this was no time to interrupt her.

Instead he sat back on the pale-washed sand of the little bay and gave himself up to the delight of this expedition, which, although completely real, had about it the quality of a dream adventure.

Other explorers discovered islands, of course, often uninhabited and unvisited ones. Only they were real places, they had always been there, simply waiting for somebody to come along and discover them. But this island was not entirely real; as lately as the day before yesterday it had not been here at all. And even now it had an air of unreality, with its sandy shores and fringe of sea enclosed in the drifting mist which shut it away from the outside world, as though it—or perhaps indeed the outside world—didn't really exist at all.

It was at this moment that he remembered his father's words, and realized with a shock of joy that his very first expedition had brought him that wonderful, rewarding 'moment of delight'.

He grinned to himself as he remembered how emphatically he had insisted that one simply could not have an adventure with the very companions with whom he was sharing this experience. He turned and looked at Linda, still stooping over her garden.

There was no trace of the spoilt little girl about her now as she followed the butterfly's progress from flower to flower, holding her breath with wonder as she studied the tremulous wings.

Ben could be seen in a shower of sand, digging a hole behind the garden. It was hard to recognize this lively, sand-spattered animal as the sleek town dog whose tailored coat hung drying in the pear tree. Even Brown Teddy looked different here, his beady eyes seeming bright with a new expression as he stared at the feather forest in Linda's garden.

As to the witch girl, he smiled to remember Linda's nick-name as Alex slid from her branch and strolled towards them, reading over what she had written as she came.

'Well, at least I've got it all jotted down,' she said, flopping down beside him with a sigh of satisfaction.

'Come and look at my garden, oh, please, you must look,' begged Linda, seizing her by the hand and dragging her to her feet again.

Alex was as delighted with the garden as Martin had been, and assured Linda that she could tell them the names of the flowers. She recognized the butterfly too.

'It's a marbled white,' she told them, and watched Martin enter it under the 'Fauna' heading. She was much impressed by the map itself, and after studying all its details she gave Martin the names of the flowers for his list. When this was done she straightened up and stood looking about her as he had done. The sun was now so high that the mist was almost dazzling in its brightness.

'It's so magical here!' she said softly. 'I wish it could just be our own little secret island and nobody else's, for ever and ever and ever.'

'Well, can't it be? We found it,' said Linda.

'Oh no. I'm sure it will have to belong to the person who owns this bit of the shore. I expect that's the Mr Williams that your trailer camp belongs to. And that will be the very worst thing that could happen to it,' she finished dejectedly.

'Why?' asked Linda.

'Because Mr Williams will turn it into a holiday attraction, I'm afraid. He'll probably arrange boat trips all through the summer months to bring visitors out here for picnics, and you know what that will mean? Paper bags, banana skins and empty tins all over our glistening sand. Oh, I wish, I wish it could stay just like this for always and never be spoilt.'

'So do I,' said Martin. 'And I don't know why it is, but even the mist helps to make it perfect in a funny sort of way.'

'Yes,' agreed Alex. 'I expect that's because it makes it feel like a dream place, miles and miles away from the world of everyday. Somehow I don't really want to see it in ordinary sunshine even, in case it mightn't look quite so magical.'

'I know just what you mean,' said Martin. 'It gives a wonderful effect, this mist-light——'

He was cut short by a throaty whine from Ben, who had grown tired of digging and now stood looking up at him expectantly.

'Oh dear, I'm afraid that means he wants his dinner; he's got his hungry look,' said Linda.

'I'd be interested to see him when he hasn't got a hungry look,' laughed Martin. 'It's lucky Mum put tins of dog food on her shopping list yesterday, or he might have had to go on having a hungry look!'

'Couldn't we all have dinner now? I'm starving too,' said Linda.

89

'I suppose we may as well,' said Martin. 'As we haven't got a watch between us, and can't even see the sun, we've no way of telling the time anyhow.'

'How grand to live on an island without any time, and just eat whenever you want to,' smiled Linda, leading the way to the boat.

'Now just a minute,' Martin called after her. 'It's no use getting too free with the food; we've got to make it last till we're rescued, remember, and that might be days if this fog doesn't clear, so we'll just have to ration ourselves, I'm afraid.'

'Ben's the lucky one; he's got enough for four whole days without any rationing,' observed Linda, climbing into the boat.

'Well, at least we've all got pears, as many as we want,' remarked Alex. 'We'd better be careful with the bread though; I don't think we'd better have more than one slice each this time.'

'We're pretty well off for meat at any rate,' said Martin. 'This corned beef is solid stuff, and it won't keep once the tin is opened, so we'll have to eat the whole lot right away.'

'Good,' murmured Linda, watching him slide the meat out of the tin and break it into three equal chunks. He arranged these on the three slices of bread that Alex had laid out in readiness.

'We can have a tomato each as well; that'll help to quench our thirst and save the drink,' he added.

'What else is there?' asked Alex.

'Corn flakes—dry of course, without any milk or sugar— potato crisps and a packet of ginger nuts——'

'Oh yes,' interrupted Linda. 'I love ginger nuts.'

90

'And a slab of cheese, but you don't like that,' he reminded her.

'I do now,' she assured him. 'I like everything here on our island.'

'Well, then, how about one ginger nut each, and a bit of cheese to follow?' suggested Alex. 'An island seems an awfully hungry place, doesn't it?'

The brief meal was over all too soon. But when Linda begged for one more ginger nut Martin was firm.

'I'm terribly sorry,' he said decidedly, 'but we've simply got to watch our food supplies; we may be here for a day or two for all we know.'

'Can I have another pear instead then?'

'Of course, have as many as you like,' said Alex. 'They won't keep anyway. Although', she added, after a moment's reflection, 'even sleepy pears might taste quite nice if one was really starving, I suppose.'

Linda reached up quickly and picked herself two pears. *She* didn't intend to be really starving if she could help it!

Alex sat with her chin on her knees, staring into the mist.

'The river's still pretty noisy,' she remarked. 'I wonder if anyone would hear us if we shouted all together?'

'Hardly,' answered Martin. 'Anyhow, they wouldn't be able to tell where the sound was coming from: fog is always so confusing. Besides, they wouldn't believe it, even if they did hear, because everyone knows there isn't really an island here at all!'

'But surely we don't want anyone to come and take us away from our lovely island?' cried Linda indignantly.

'Well, it's all right *so* far,' admitted Alex cautiously.

91

CHAPTER 9

ALEX curled up in the boat with her notebook, re-reading
what she had written, changing a word here and a sentence
there, and generally tidying up the whole account, which had
been written so fast that it was all but illegible in places.

Martin climbed into the tree above her with some vague idea
of keeping watch. But since the mist made it impossible to see
more than a yard or two beyond the island shore he soon gave
up the attempt. Instead he pulled out his pencil, and like Alex
began to tidy up his morning's work, making a neat new copy
of his map. Linda climbed on to the branch beside him, but
after watching him for a moment or two she tucked Brown
Teddy into the waistband of her shorts and crawled away
through the branches, whispering as she went.

'Careful how you go,' warned Martin. 'Don't climb out
where the branches hang over the water, will you?'

'I won't,' she promised. 'Brown Teddy and I only want to go into all the rooms in our pear-tree house again, so's we'll be able to remember them for always, even when we're quite grown up. Then we can come back here for secret adventures when we're in bed at night. Now—this one is the laundry . . .' As she spoke her voice sank into the curious whispering sing-song tone in which her adventure-talks with Brown Teddy were always carried on.

In an hour she was back, demanding tea.

'Don't be silly, you can't possibly be hungry yet,' objected Martin. He would have said it even more emphatically if he had known that it was only eleven o'clock in the morning— not yet lunch time in the world beyond the mist!

'Please!' she wheedled. 'I really *am* hungry.'

'What is there left in the way of food, Alex?' he called down. 'We don't want to open another tin yet. Is there anything else she can have?'

'Bread, jam and dry corn flakes if she likes them.'

'And cheese and ginger nuts,' prompted Linda.

'Oh, very well then, I suppose we may as well,' said Martin, surprised to discover that he himself was also beginning to feel quite hungry, now that he came to think of it.

When Ben saw them eating he decided he was hungry too. But Martin had no intention of opening another of his tins yet, since he never had more than one a day at home. Instead he gave him a drink of water, measuring it carefully into the bailer from the almost empty flask. The little dog gulped it down, then looked up for more. Seeing Martin hesitate he whined beseechingly. Martin poured out the final inch reluctantly.

'That's all there is,' he said, a note of anxiety creeping into

his voice in spite of his effort to hide it. Alex looked up quickly
but said nothing.

Ben, however, did say something. He had no sooner licked
up the final drop than he raised his head suspiciously and a low
growl rumbled in his throat.

'Ben! Darling Benbow, whatever is the matter?' cried
Linda, dropping down from the tree to fling her arms round

his neck. But Ben was in no mood for cuddling, and shaking himself free of her he ran to the extreme edge of the water, where he began to bark into the mist in short, sharp bursts, hackles bristling into a ridge along his back.

'He must have heard something out there in the mist,' said Alex. 'Perhaps it's somebody coming to look for us. Let's all shout together and see if we get any answer.'

They joined their shouts to Ben's next burst of barking, then held their breaths to listen, half fancying they heard an answering shout, although the noise of the river made it impossible to be sure. They tried again, but heard nothing further, and presently Ben himself lost interest in whatever had aroused him.

In some strange way Ben's barking had broken the spell of the island. 'I wonder what time it is anyway,' said Martin restlessly. His thoughts were all of his mother now, and he wished the mist would clear so that there might be a chance of getting back to set her mind at rest.

Alex returned to the boat and sat down to make a copy of Martin's map for herself, while Linda wandered away to her garden. Martin knelt on the sand, examining the chinks in the boat's planking, wondering whether it might be possible to patch her up sufficiently to carry them as far as the shore. He was worried by their rapidly dwindling store of food and drink, and knew that before very long they would be forced to try to leave the island if nobody came to rescue them. He got up and wandered along the tide-line, picking up any oddments he could find, with the idea of trying to plug the cracks in the boat's sides.

He returned with his hands full of seaweed and uprooted grass, together with some scraps of cloth and paper disentangled

95

from the wreckage washed against the tree. Lying down beside the boat he began systematically plugging any crack he could find. It was an awkward job, and he wriggled as far underneath the boat as he could get, packing his odd bits of stuffing into the crevices with determined fingers. Time slipped by and the island became very quiet, with no sound to be heard but the steady rush of the river hurrying past.

Ben's explosive bark burst into this silence like a bomb. Martin sprang up and saw at once that this time something really was exciting the little dog, making him so far forget his dislike of getting wet that he had actually bounced out from

the shore into several inches of water. Here he stood with his tail stiff and hackles raised, barking frantically.

Martin swooped on him, and holding him firmly with one hand closed his mouth forcibly with the other.

'Hush, Ben! Shut up and let me listen,' he commanded. Despite the dog's smothered yelps it was now possible to listen for outside sounds. And almost at once there was a sound, a human shout rising distinctly above the noise of the river.

Alex and Martin shouted in reply and Linda ran up to join them, staring at the fog in open-mouthed amazement as though she really had forgotten that there was another world outside their island.

Releasing Ben, Martin shouted again, while Ben himself made up for lost time, barking more furiously than before. When he stopped for breath the children listened intently. Hearing no sound they called again, but the silence continued.

'They've gone away—I'm glad,' said Linda.

But Martin and Alex were old enough to realize that this island life could not go on for ever, and that if the whole adventure were not to be spoilt by thirst and hunger they must be rescued soon. Martin remembered that his father had mentioned hardship, but he shied away from the thought today, since they had Linda with them, and she was obviously far too young for hardship. Leaning forward into the mist he called again:

'Ahoy there! Who are you?'

Ben whined eagerly, then suddenly wagged his tail as a vague shape loomed through the mist.

'A boat!' shouted Martin.

'It's the ferry-boat, and there's Old Joseph himself—oh, and

Janet too!' cried Alex, running into the water to seize the bow
of the boat as it grounded on the sand.

'*Alex!*' breathed Janet, too amazed to say anything more.

'Well—I'm—jiggered!' exploded Old Joseph, looking
slowly from one face to another. Then shaking his head in
bewilderment he continued:

'Well, it's Janet you've got to thank, Janet and that there
dog! She made me come, insisted she could hear a dog barking
here although I kept telling her there weren't no place out here
in the estuary where any dog could be.'

'I was afraid some poor animal had got stranded out here on
some of the wreckage washed down the river yesterday,' Janet
explained.

Her father's bewildered gaze had wandered from the children to the sandbank on which they stood.

'But where have we got to anyway?' he demanded in a puzzled tone. 'There wasn't never no land out here before, and I've known this estuary all my life. Seems like it can't be real land somehow.'

'Well, the people on it are real enough!' Janet pointed out.

'Ah, that's true!' replied her father, coming out of his reverie with a jerk. 'So you'd better hop in, all of you, in case the whole place might vanish away as mysteriously as it came.'

'Oh, but we can't go and leave our darling island,' cried Linda, stepping back. 'Oh, please, Martin, let's stay.'

'I'm afraid we'll have to go, Lin,' he said, putting a gentle but determined hand on her shoulder. 'Got Brown Teddy safely?'

She nodded, blinking back the sudden tears as she allowed herself to be lifted into the boat, while Alex hoisted Ben over the side.

'I must just collect the provisions and my haversack,' said Martin, turning back.

'And my writing things—they're in the boat,' Alex called after him.

'And Ben's coat—it's in the airing-cupboard,' shouted Linda.

'Come along now, make haste, for goodness' sake,' called the old ferryman. 'I'll be thankful to get off from here and that's a fact. I don't rightly know where I am any more, what with the mist and the shifting sands and all.'

After a final hasty glance around the island Martin splashed back to the ferry-boat and scrambled on board with his load.

'Ready?' said the old man, and with a powerful pull on his

starboard oar he swung the heavy old craft about and began to pull upstream with long deliberate strokes. Keeping his eyes fixed on the water, he took his direction from the current flowing past, since the mist was still too dense to allow him to see as as far the shore.

They were a silent boatload. The three castaways sat watching their island fade into the mist as though it had never been. When its shadowy outline finally disappeared, the slow tears rolled down Linda's cheeks, although she made no sound. The others were equally silent, while Janet sat deep in a dream of her own, realizing that this eventful trip could be worked up into an exciting feature for tomorrow's edition of her paper.

After ten minutes' steady rowing Old Joseph pulled out of the main stream into the creek. There was less current here, and his task was easier, giving him time to think. His blue eyes lost their twinkle and his voice was unusually grave as he remarked:

'Wind's getting up. There'll be a big old tide coming up the estuary tonight, with the wind blowing from this quarter.'

Janet glanced up quickly and caught his eye. She didn't speak, but Martin noticed her arm tighten suddenly around Linda, who was sitting beside her.

As they neared the ferry cottage the old man turned to Alex.

'No sense landing you at your place,' he told her. 'Mrs Challenor's not back yet—she spent the night in town on account of the storm.'

'Just as well, since she believes you're safe at Mrs Simpson's,' observed Janet drily.

'You'd best stay with us till she returns,' continued the old man. 'I'll row you over as soon as ever we hear the taxi coming down the lane.'

'I'll have to go over later myself in any case,' announced Janet. 'I'll be going round to the office as soon as I've got this story sorted out.'

Martin's heart thumped uncomfortably as his thoughts returned unwillingly to his mother. What sort of state would she be in, he wondered. It was only too easy to imagine, and when they reached the ferry steps he was the first to scramble ashore.

Turning quickly to Old Joseph, he held out his hand.

'Thank you most terrifically for coming to rescue us,' he said. 'We'll bring Mum down here to see you later on. I know she'll want to thank you herself as well. But now would you mind if we run? I'm afraid she may be in a bit of a state about us, you see.'

'Ah—you run,' said the old man, nodding understandingly.

Even Linda realized the urgency of the moment, and grabbing her share of their belongings she called to Ben and stumbled up through the steep woods, doing her best to keep pace with her brother's rapid strides.

Half way up the hillside they heard a great whoop and looked up to see Rocky bounding down through the trees.

'Everyone's looking for you!' he shouted, crashing excitedly through the undergrowth to meet them.

Martin pushed on faster than ever, wasting no breath on questions. But Rocky was only too ready to do all the talking.

'They've even got the police on it now,' he informed them. 'Only, what with the bridge washed away and the telephones out of order, they only just got word to them. And, anyway, nobody knew you was lost till your mum got back this morning.'

'This morning?' echoed Martin in astonishment, pausing a moment for Linda to catch up. 'But why this morning?'

'Well, the bridge was gone like I said, so they tried to get round by the mountain road. But even up there the streams were flooded, pouring all over the place, till they couldn't even see where the road was supposed to be. So in the end they had to abandon the car and walk all the way round by the new bridge, miles and miles that is, and never a car all night to give them a lift. We was having breakfast when they walked into the camp.'

'Oh, poor Mum!' cried Martin, hurrying on again, dragging Linda along by the hand. Rocky fell into step beside them, and although he was getting short of breath he still managed to go on talking.

''Course your mum thought you'd be with Mr Palmer,' he went on. 'And Mr Palmer thought you'd all gone off in the car —Mrs Palmer told him you was going when she went in to get his tea. When he heard the bridge was down he tried to phone, but the lines were dead by then. So he guessed you'd all have to put up in town overnight; somebody told us the mountain road was impassable for cars.

'And you're not the only ones missing, neither,' he informed them. 'They went down to ask old Joseph if he'd seen you, and he's gone too, and his boat, though they may find that when the mist clears, of course.'

Although he now had almost no breath left Rocky was still prepared to go on talking. But as they reached the top of the hill Martin let go of Linda's hand and raced ahead to the camp.

For a long while Mrs Roberts sat on the step of the trailer, clutching her children as though she would never let them go, while Martin poured out the story of the night's adventure. And now it was Rocky who was silent as he listened spellbound to the description of the island. At the end he heaved a tremendous sigh.

'Gee!' he breathed enviously. 'That was a smashing adventure all right! You're lucky, you are, nobody in the Adventure Club ever had an adventure that big.' And then in a rush he went on: 'Look, how about you coming down to the hide-out tonight and giving us a lecture about it, you know, like a guest speaker? We could even have a glass of water for you, like they do at Dad's council meetings back home.'

Martin felt very much the real explorer, back from foreign parts, as he accepted this flattering invitation.

They might have stayed talking a good deal longer if Ben hadn't interrupted the conversation, doing his best to explain by means of throaty whines that his drinking bowl was not in its usual corner.

'Oh, how thoughtless of me!' exclaimed the children's mother, glancing guiltily at her watch. 'You poor darlings, you must be starving. Come along and we'll see about lunch.'

'Lunch?' echoed Linda, open-eyed. 'But, Mum, we had lunch simply hours ago. We've even had tea since then.'

'What time is it anyway?' asked Martin curiously.

'Nearly one o'clock,' replied his mother.

Linda was surprised to discover that in spite of what she had just said, she was as hungry for lunch as usual. When she had finished she put down her spoon and fork with a satisfied smile and remarked: 'They'll never believe me at school when I tell them we had two lunches and two teas in the same day!'

'I suppose there just isn't such a thing as time on an island like ours,' mused Martin reflectively.

CHAPTER 10

EVEN Ben slept late next morning, and the sun was already
high in the sky by the time they had breakfast in the trailer.

They were just finishing the last of the morning jobs when
there was a tap on the door and there stood Alex. She was
obviously bubbling over with excitement, but she managed to
hold it in check while Martin introduced her to his mother.

'Ah, I've been longing to meet the third member of the
expedition,' smiled Mrs Roberts. 'I was so sorry you'd gone by
the time I called at the ferry cottage yesterday afternoon.'

'I went back with Janet,' explained Alex. 'She had to go
back to her office to do *this*!' and with a flourish she produced a
battered newspaper, limp with constant folding and re-folding.
Opening it she spread it on the table under the window,
standing back so that the others could get near.

'Martin!' shrieked Linda. 'That's a picture of your map
what you drew of our island! Look, it even says "Linda's
Garden" where you wrote it in tiny little letters.'

106

But Martin's attention had been caught by the headline above the map:

ISLAND ADVENTURE

Children stranded overnight on sandbank

His eye ran down the column, in which Janet had outlined the events which led to their landing on the island. The paragraph concluded: 'From here the story shall be told in the words of one of the participants in the adventure, eleven-year-old Alex Stephenson, who wrote the following eye-witness account on the spot:

'"It was a new island," she tells us. "Only that day its sandy top had risen out of the river whose foaming currents raced by on either side ..."'

Martin read on rapidly. When he came to the foot of the page he swung round excitedly.

'Why, Alex, this is absolutely marvellous!' he cried. 'You have really got the feel and the sound of the island here, just exactly the way it was.'

'Did Alex write all this printing in the paper herself?' demanded Linda, looking from one to the other. When Martin nodded she cried delightedly:

'Oh, Alex, they said you'd never get your writing published —and now you have!'

'Well, Janet helped of course,' said Alex.

'Helped, yes, by taking the stuff to her editor,' said Martin. 'But Janet didn't write all this: how could she? She didn't hear the migrant birds calling in the darkness or see their little footprints on the tide-line.'

Alex flushed with pleasure at his appreciation. Then turning back to the paper she remarked:

'Even Ben has got himself into print. Look over here where Janet says it was his barking that attracted her attention, and sent her to fetch her father.'

'Good old Benbow,' murmured Martin. 'I used to call him a sissy dog, but if it hadn't been for him we might never have been rescued at all, I suppose——' He pulled himself up sharply, aware that it was best not to say this sort of thing in front of his mother. But fortunately she was still bending over the table, absorbed in the newspaper story.

'This account is extremely well written, Alex,' she commented. 'It sounds a lovely island from your description. I don't like the way you got there, though, not one bit.'

'Oh it was quite safe really,' Martin put in quickly. 'That pear tree would never have sunk in a hundred years: a tree like that never would, you know. And our boat was so tangled up in its branches that it couldn't have gone down either.'

'I wonder,' said his mother very quietly.

'How about showing this paper to the Palmers? They might be interested, I should think,' suggested Martin, anxious to remove that look from his mother's face. To his relief she smiled and picked up the paper.

'You're right, they'd like to see it,' she agreed. 'I'll bring it back to you straight away, of course. You'll be wanting to show it to Rocky, I'm sure.'

'Yes, and we must get an extra copy to send to Dad,' said Martin.

'Oh, good, then he'll be able to see that lovely map with my garden in it,' said Linda.

108

'Yes, I'd like him to see that map,' said Martin. 'And even more I want him to see what Alex has written about the island itself. He always told me that exploring was something more than just excitement and adventure. When he reads what Alex says he'll know that we really did find our moment of delight.'

'Moment of delight,' repeated Alex thoughtfully. 'I think that must have been when we heard the birds all calling in the darkness.'

'I think it was when the butterfly came flittering over my garden,' said Linda decidedly.

Martin remembered the pale curve of the island bay and the sparkles of its rippled waves muted under the mist-light. He knew this scene would linger in his memory as something to delight him all his life, but he felt incapable of putting it into words.

'Let's go out to the end of the headland and look at the island, shall we?' suggested Alex. 'We'll be able to see it now the mist has cleared.'

They climbed over the gate at the end of the field and set off along the ridge of the headland. It was a mellow September morning, the sunlight still a little hazy after the mist. The winding river was softly blue, flowing through sands that looked almost pink in the pearly light. They walked out to the extreme end of the headland, to a point from which they could look down on the cove with its battered boathouse and ruined cottage.

But just off-shore, where the island should have been, there was nothing to be seen but a tumble of white-capped waves. The island itself had completely disappeared.

'It can't have gone!' cried Alex in dismay. 'Not with the tree and the boat and everything, it simply can't!'

But it *had* gone. The tree and the boat had been swept out to sea on the night tide, leaving the sandy island unprotected in the tideway. No sooner was its breakwater gone than a small ripple slid over the sand, to be followed by more persistent waves. By the time the tide began to ebb the two-day island had disappeared, vanishing under the water as mysteriously as it had appeared a couple of days ago.

Martin reached for Linda's hand.

'That makes it an even bigger adventure than we realized,' he said unsteadily. 'Better not let Mum know the island has gone if we can help it.'

At his words Linda pulled her hand from his, and flinging

herself face downwards on the grass she burst into a storm of tears.

'It's gone!' she wailed. 'Our darling little island's gone and we'll never see it again.'

For a long while her sobs were the only sound to be heard on the quiet headland, as the other two stared thoughtfully down on the tumbled water flowing over the spot on which they had so recently been stranded.

Martin was the first to speak.

'You know I think it's rather a nice way for it to end,' he said slowly.

'Nice?' Linda raised a shocked face, streaked with tears which she swept away with an impatient hand.

'Yes,' he replied, sitting down beside her. 'You see, we couldn't have kept the island anyway. We'd have to go home and leave it for other explorers to find and call their own.'

'And another thing,' said Alex. 'We'd never, never have been allowed to go out there again by ourselves, that's quite certain. There'd always have to be a grown-up with us, and very soon it would have been everybody's island.'

'But as things are it can't be claimed or spoilt by anyone, ever,' Martin pointed out.

Alex sat down beside them, clasping her arms about her knees.

'And to think that we are the only people who ever landed there!' she said softly. 'And, except for Janet and Old Joseph, the only people in all the world who ever saw it even—or ever will see it now, of course.'

Linda's sobs lessened as she considered this.

'So it's really turned into a secret place of our private own after all,' she observed. 'Like when me and Brown Teddy have secret adventures in bed at night. Only this was a secret adventure and a real one too, wasn't it?'

Alex nodded thoughtfully.

'Yes, it's—well, it's rather like a dream come true,' she said.

'Or true come dream,' said Martin slowly. 'Because although it's true, it's also something that will stay with us all as a dream for the rest of our lives.' He spoke hesitantly, not quite knowing how to put his thoughts into words.

But Alex was gazing out over the water with shining eyes.

'What a lovely idea,' she mused. 'Some day, not yet, but some day, when I'm ready, I shall make that idea into a book.'

'What will the book be called?' demanded Linda.

'*September Island*, I expect,' said Alex.

About the Author

Rosalie Fry was born on Vancouver Island, Canada, and during World War II she was stationed in the Orkney Islands where she was a Cypher Officer in the Women's Royal Naval Service. She has traveled extensively in Europe, and now makes her home in Swansea, South Wales.

She is an artist as well as an author, and has illustrated many of her books. Before her writing and drawing began taking up most of her time, she was a well-known creator of children's toys. Her love of country life and travel is reflected in her books for young people, which include *Secret of the Ron Mor Skerry*, *The Echo Song*—both of which were Junior Literary Guild selections—and *The Riddle of the Figurehead*, her most recent book.